WILD RIVIERA

TYSON WILD BOOK THREE

TRIPP ELLIS

WELCOME

Want more books like this?

You'll probably never hear about my new releases unless you join my newsletter.

SIGN UP HERE

1

_____

The names and locations have been fictionalized to protect the innocent, and the guilty.

I t was, by far, the strangest flight I had ever been on. No, we didn't see a UFO, we weren't abducted by aliens, we didn't get sucked into a vortex and travel through time.

But it was equally as exciting.

I'll get to the good stuff in a minute.

First, the crap.

The flight was delayed an hour and a half.

Fine.

Whatever.

Not a big deal.

Airport food has gotten better these days, and there are

some surprisingly decent options in the terminal. And hey, *people watching*.

When the jetway finally opened, I boarded the plane first—the benefits of *Premier Access*. Flying coach sucks, and I wasn't about to do it on an international flight.

First Class all the way, baby.

I rolled my baggage down the gangway, greeted the smiling blonde flight attendant, stuffed my small roller bag into the overhead compartment, and took a seat.

The plush leather was comfortable, had lots of legroom, and the seat was wide enough for an actual person to sit in. And it reclined far enough that I might actually get a descent nap.

The perky flight attendant took my drink order as other passengers were boarding. She introduced herself as Amanda and begged me to let her know if there was anything she could do to make my flight more enjoyable.

I could think of a few things, but I kept my thoughts to myself.

She had bright eyes and a cheery smile that belonged in a toothpaste commercial. The tight, fitted skirt would be a welcome view for the next 10 hours.

I hoped I would be able to sleep for the entire flight and arrive rested, but that wasn't going to be the case.

The attendant brought me a Diet Coke, and I realized that was probably a bad choice because of the caffeine. But a few glasses of whiskey and a sleeping pill might do the trick.

I was no stranger to international flights. I knew if I timed it just right, I could avoid most of the jet lag. I had picked an evening flight for just that reason. But sleeping on a plane was never my specialty. Too many interruptions. Cramped seats that never seemed to recline far enough. I hoped that First Class would alleviate some of those common problems.

The flight introduction video looped on the headrest monitor in front of me, welcoming me in 37 different languages.

Passengers filtered onto the 777, and I prayed to the travel gods that no screaming children sat next to me. I wasn't in the mood to deal with their piercing screeches or poopy diapers.

I brought earplugs just in case.

I settled in and watched people fumble with their bags, banging them into my shoulder as they trudged down the aisle.

I felt the disapproving stares of the coach passengers as they strolled through the First Class section, looking at me like some type of privileged asshole. I wasn't privileged at all. I paid for this seat with my hard-earned money. Okay, maybe it wasn't so *hard-earned*. I used my poker winnings. And money won in poker was twice as sweet.

Then the first of two strange occurrences happened.

A woman boarded the plane wearing a designer sundress, a wide-brimmed hat, and oversized sunglasses.

The flight attendants fawned all over her.

She had gorgeous, tanned legs and a svelte form. I couldn't

see much of her face behind the sunglasses, but what did show was nothing short of perfection. Sculpted cheekbones, full lips, and radiant skin.

All eyes fell upon her, and a hushed murmur of gossip filtered about the cabin.

The woman had a certain magnetism about her.

Then I realized why.

Before I knew it, she was standing at the edge of my seat, looking at her ticket, comparing it to the seat number on the overhead bin.

I realized that was my cue to stand.

I unbuckled my safety belt and climbed out of my seat so she could slip into her seat by the window.

I don't do window seats.

I *always* have to sit in the aisle.

I need to be able to get up and move at will. Sure, you have to get up every time somebody wants to go to the lavatory, but it beats being crammed against the window.

Fortunately, I won the seat-mate lottery.

I settled back into my chair after *Miss Magnetic* took hers. People sitting around us kept staring. It was a little awkward.

I don't usually get nervous, but when I realized who the woman sitting next to me was, my heart started beating a little faster. A thrill of excitement vibrated through my body. My palms grew sweaty.

I was sitting next to *Bree Taylor*.

Yes, THAT Bree Taylor.

The biggest movie star on the planet!

I had seen her in one of those summer blockbuster super-hero movies where she pranced around the screen in a skintight bodysuit that looked painted on. She kicked ass and delivered snarky one-liners. And posters of her in the suit were plastered on every teenage boy's wall across the country.

She also won an Academy Award® the previous year for a dramatic role in a film that nobody ever saw.

Her breakthrough was a big comedy hit about a group of girls who go to Vegas for a bachelor party. But after the bride hits her head in a freak accident, she wakes up with no memory of her fiancé. The girls have 24 hours to get the bride to fall back in love with her fiancé and say *I do* at the altar. Trouble is, she's fallen for someone else.

But, it's not like I *really* followed her career, or anything.

Okay, who am I bullshitting? I'm a big fan. I mean, who wouldn't be a fan of hers. She's gorgeous. She has an infectious personality on screen, and you just can't take your eyes off of her.

I felt like a little schoolboy with a crush.

Part of me wanted to start talking to her instantly. But my rational mind said *keep your mouth shut before you say something stupid.*

I've always tried not to meet celebrities. The times I have, I've always been disappointed. They can never live up to the idea you create in your head. I was worried that Bree might be rude and snotty if I tried to instigate a conversation, so I pretended not to notice her. And let me tell you, I should have gotten an *Academy Fucking Award*® for that performance.

People kept boarding the plane, and the overhead bins were getting full. Some jackass tried to stuff an oversized case in the overhead and kept slamming the compartment, trying to get it shut.

There was no way in hell it would ever fit. A moron could see that. But this guy kept trying.

Finally an attendant came by, took the bag, and gate checked it—much to the passenger's displeasure.

Once everyone was aboard, they sealed the doors, and the safety video began playing. I'd seen the damn thing a thousand times before, so I tuned out. I grabbed the sky catalog and looked for useless items that I just *had to have*—all the while trying to think of a good opener.

Nothing I came up with sounded satisfactory to me.

The plane pushed back from the jetway, and we taxied down the runway. The pilot crackled over the loudspeaker, informing us of another delay, but assured us we'd be in the air within 15 minutes.

I didn't really mind the delay. As long as we didn't lose an engine during flight, I was cool. Besides, I had the best seat on the plane. 10 hours in a chair next to Bree Taylor didn't seem so bad.

Before long, we rocketed down the runway and lifted into the air. Those first few moments of liftoff always seem a little precarious. The aircraft pitched and rolled slightly, and hydraulics whirred as the landing gear retracted.

I'd flown in C-17 transports that were so loaded down it was a miracle we ever got airborne—taking off and landing on tiny tarmacs in remote locations across the globe with runways far too short for comfort.

Commercial air travel didn't phase me anymore.

Shortly after we reached cruising altitude, the captain's voice crackled over the intercom, telling us we had smooth skies ahead, and he would turn off the fasten seatbelt sign. A moment later, the buzzer dinged, and the indicator light went off.

It wasn't long after that when a barrage of fans approached.

A woman brought her young daughter down the aisle and hovered over my seat, ignoring my personal space. "I'm sorry to bother you, but my daughter is such a huge fan. Could she get your autograph?"

"Sure," Bree said with a smile. She looked at the little girl and asked, "What's your name?"

"Maggie," the girl replied with a soft, awestruck voice.

Bree had a sharpie handy for just such an occasion.

The little girl handed her a children's book, and Bree signed it. It was the only thing the girl had to write on.

Bree smiled and handed the book back.

The little girl looked delighted.

Her mother asked, "Would it be okay if we get a picture?"

"Sure. No problem."

I unbuckled my seatbelt and climbed into the aisle as the woman and her daughter nearly trampled me. They sat next to Bree, and the woman handed me her cell phone. "Would you mind?"

I snapped the picture and handed the phone back to her.

The woman thanked Bree once again and took her daughter back to coach.

This scenario repeated itself for another 20 minutes as various passengers just *had* to get an autograph and a picture. It went on until the flight attendant pushed a serving cart down the aisle, blocking off First Class.

"Doesn't that get annoying?" I asked.

It wasn't a line. It wasn't an opener. It just came out of my mouth without a thought.

Bree smiled. "I don't mind, really. It's what I signed up for. I wouldn't be where I am today if people didn't go see my movies. There was a time when I couldn't book an acting job to save my soul. I know it's not going to last forever, so I might as well enjoy the ride."

It was a refreshing attitude, and I was relieved she wasn't a snotty little brat. I wouldn't have been able to watch her movies anymore if she was.

"What's your name?" she asked.

"Tyson."

We shook hands. Her hand was soft and delicate. I felt like I'd been touched by an angel.

"Nice to meet you, Tyson. I'm Bree."

As if I didn't know what her name was.

Her infectious smile dazzled me. It was probably all just an act, but she seemed genuine.

The second strange thing about the flight happened next.

2

"Why are you flying commercial? Don't you have your own airplane?" I asked.

She chuckled. "I wish."

"Didn't you make like $20 million for your last picture? Not that I keep up with that kind of stuff. But, aren't you a big baller?"

"My financial manager says I need to scale back my purchases. I really don't think I spend that much, but it goes quick."

I arched a curious eyebrow at her.

"The agent takes 10%, the manager takes 15%, my attorney takes 5%. Half goes to taxes. I've got a house in LA, a condo in New York, a boat in Monaco, several pieces of fine art, and lots of dresses and shoes."

I laughed. "That must be a hell of a monthly nut?"

"Too much." She smiled. "You only live once, right?"

I gave a nod of agreement.

"It's only money," she sighed.

"It's *only money* when you have it. When you don't, it's like trying to survive without oxygen."

"True."

We hit a little patch of turbulence that rattled the bulkheads and shook the seats. There were a few gasps and groans about the cabin.

"Do you ever miss being a normal person?" I asked.

Her sunglasses had long since come off, and she looked at me with her piercing blue eyes. There was a subtle smirk on her plump lips. "Whatever do you mean?" she asked, coyly. "I am a normal person. I'm just your average, everyday girl."

She knew damn good and well she wasn't.

I chuckled again. "There's nothing average about you."

"Hey, I put my pants on one leg at a time, just like everybody else. I drink beer, watch my favorite shows, curse in traffic. I have good days and bad days. Sometimes I even pick my nose and fart." She laughed.

I was stunned by her response. "Yes, but I'm sure you look glamorous when you do it."

She smiled. "The only thing I miss is the lack of privacy. My life isn't mine anymore. It's everybody else's. It would be fun to sneak out and go to the store or to a movie or to a club without having a gaggle of photographers follow me around. I can do that more in Europe than I can in the United States. In Los Angeles, I'm hounded."

"Well, I've been chatting your ear off for the last hour and haven't given you any privacy. My apologies," I said. "I'm sure the last thing you need is some idiot asking you questions about what it's like to be a celebrity."

She put her hand on my forearm and smiled, "I don't mind. Really. Our conversation has been refreshing. Everybody always wants something from me. They want me to read a script, do a movie, endorse a product, help their career, loan them money... And whatever I do for someone, it's never good enough." She paused, then smiled again. "You haven't even asked me for my autograph."

"Keep smiling at me like that, and I might ask you out on a date."

She looked curious. "Now, that's interesting. Nobody ever asks me out on a date."

My eyes narrowed at her with doubt. "I find that hard to believe."

"Usually, if they are a celebrity, they have their PR person call my PR person. Or their agent calls my agent and sets up a *meeting*," she said with air quotes. "And you wouldn't believe the number of dick pics guys send me on social media."

I laughed. "I can imagine."

There was a brief pause. I worried that the conversation was going to end. I scrambled for something witty to say.

"So, what do you do for a living?" she asked.

Not an easy question to answer.

I was heading halfway across the globe to do something I

swore I would never do again—assassinate a man. A rogue agent who had shot me and left me for dead in Mexico.

Not my favorite person. Agent Cartwright.

I'd been to hell and back. Literally. I danced with the devil. I felt the heat and smelled the stench and had gotten a taste of eternal damnation. A few moments were more than enough for me.

But I had gotten a second chance at life, and I swore I wasn't going to make the same mistakes. I'd been searching for redemption, but I kept finding myself in the same old situations.

What did I do for a living?

I pondered the question for a long moment.

"I keep telling myself I'm retired. But somehow I keep taking clients," I said, trying to choose my words carefully.

"You're too young to be retired," Bree said. "Unless you're one of those tech guys who's made a bazillion dollars by 30?"

I chuckled. "No. Not a bazillion."

We chatted for hours, and my plan to get sleep went out the window. I didn't mind. I'd sleep when I was dead. Right now, I was alive, and she was easy to talk to.

During the middle of the flight, a man sitting toward the back of the First Class section stood up and grabbed the perky flight attendant as she walked by.

In the blink of an eye, he had his arm around her throat, and he pulled a small bottle that looked like nasal spray from his pocket. He held it in the air and shouted something about a toxin and how we'd all die if we didn't comply with his demands.

The cabin was dim. The sky outside the windows was black. Most of the passengers were in a stupor—groggy from half-assed slumber, wrapped in thin blankets with tiny pillows that were barely larger than a marshmallow wedged under their heads. It took them a moment to realize we were being hijacked with a bottle of nasal spray.

Fucking *nasal spray!*

Bree's eyes widened, and she gripped my forearm tight.

"Just stay calm," I whispered. "Everything's going to be all right."

I had no idea what was in the spray bottle, but like everyone else on board, my imagination was running wild.

Anthrax?

A viral pathogen?

Perhaps a nerve agent?

It was a crude delivery system, but a few pumps would surely put enough into the air to affect a number of passengers in First Class. The air recirculation system could quickly disperse it through the fuselage.

The general public had seen enough movies, and watched enough media coverage, of anthrax and chemical attacks to buy into the plausibility of the scenario. Hell, in the back of my mind I thought, it could just be *nasal spray* and nothing more. Saline? An antihistamine?

But nobody wanted to take any chances.

The terrorist pulled the flight attendant toward the front of the cabin. His eyes locked on Bree as he passed by. He knew he had a high-value hostage. It gave him considerable bargaining power.

I scanned the cabin looking for accomplices. Surely this man wasn't acting alone?

3

A man sitting toward the back of the plane climbed out of his seat and marched down the aisle. He pulled a gun from a concealed holster and aimed it at the terrorist. "US Air Marshal. Let the flight attendant go, and put the weapon down!"

Adrenaline coursed through my veins. I had a bad feeling about the scenario.

I glanced around, looking for another Air Marshal, but no one revealed themself. I knew the Air Marshals were stretched pretty thin, and they usually traveled in pairs, but it wouldn't be out of the realm of possibility to have a single marshal on an international flight.

As the Air Marshal advanced down the aisle, nearing the First Class cabin, another terrorist sprang from a seat behind him and attacked. This man was a trained professional. He moved with precision. He kicked the back of the Air Marshal's knees, bringing him down to the deck. In a continuous fluid motion, the terrorist grabbed the man's arm, and slid his hand up to the barrel of the weapon, twisting it 180°, snapping the Air Marshal's finger in the trigger guard. An elbow to the back of the neck flattened the Air Marshal on the deck, and the terrorist had the weapon clean.

He aimed the barrel of the Sig P250 at the Air Marshal's back, and his finger squeezed the trigger. Muzzle flash flickered from the barrel, and a loud bang echoed throughout the fuselage.

The bullet impacted the Air Marshal, spraying a geyser of blood. The projectile probably snapped his spine. The marshal was dead, instantly.

We didn't lose cabin pressure, so I could only assume the bullet didn't penetrate the deck on exiting the body.

The terrified screeches of the passengers filled the cabin.

This was no joke, and the terrorists wanted everyone to know they weren't fucking around. It was a display of force. An attempt to discourage anyone else from getting any ideas about being a hero.

By this time, sweat was beading on the forehead of the nasal spray terrorist. He had moved with the flight attendant toward the front of the cabin and was in the galley near the cockpit. His eyes were wide, and he seemed a little frazzled.

The man who disarmed the Air Marshal seemed calm, cool, and collected. He advanced down the aisle and shouted, "Stay in your seats and no one else will get hurt. Comply with our demands and there will be no more bloodshed. I will not hesitate to kill anyone on this flight who causes trouble."

The man with the gun moved down the aisle toward me. I had a few seconds to come up with a plan. There was no doubt that the pilot was aware of the situation and had squawked a 7500 to air traffic control, letting them know that a hijacking was in progress.

I could feel the aircraft slow and drop altitude. We were far enough along that I wasn't sure if we would turn back and head to Miami, or keep going to Nice? If the terrorists got their way, who knows where we'd be headed?

I had unbuckled my safety harness when this all began. As the man with the gun passed by, I elbowed him in the groin and launched to my feet, grabbing the pistol, aiming it toward the ceiling. I stripped the weapon from his hand, and elbowed him in the face, smashing his nose. Crimson blood splattered, and he tumbled back, crashing down. Two other passengers pounced on him as I spun around and took aim at the terrorist with the nasal spray.

"Put the gun down, or we all die!" he shouted, his eyes full of fear.

He used the flight attendant as a shield—his left arm around her throat, his right hand holding the nasal spray in front of her.

I kept the weapon aimed at his right shoulder. It was the only fully exposed part of his body, along with the edge of his face. It was a tight shot, even on steady ground. But at 30,000 feet, hitting a small patch of turbulence could make for a bad day.

The terrorist hesitated.

I could see it in his eyes—he was petrified. He either didn't want to release the toxin, or there was no toxin at all?

I was about to call his bluff when the flight attended elbowed him in his man-bits and spun from his grasp.

I had a clear shot, and I took it.

The deafening bang of the pistol filled the First Class cabin as I squeezed the trigger. Muzzle flash flickered from the barrel, and the bullet tore across the compartment and smacked into the terrorist's shoulder. The force of impact knocked him against the bulkhead, and the nasal spray dropped to the deck, instantly—the brachial plexus (the nerves in the shoulder) shredded beyond repair. He'd never make a fist again—if the arm was even salvageable.

Blood painted the bulkheads, and the terrorist writhed in agony on the ground.

I moved forward and scooped the nasal spray from the deck. I kept my weapon aimed at the terrorist as the flight attendants found restraints they had on board just in case of a scenario like this. They bound the man about the wrists and ankles as he screamed in pain. I instructed the flight attendant to find a sealable container for the nasal spray.

A Ziploc bag would have to do. It wasn't the ideal scenario. Now it was just a matter of time to see if anyone had been affected by the toxin.

As far as I could tell, the terrorist had never actuated the pump spray.

A flight attendant grabbed a pile of cloth napkins and applied pressure to the man's wounds. Another flight attendant asked if there was a doctor onboard, her voice crackling over the intercom. A First Class passenger made his way forward to the galley and attended to the man.

Once the situation was under control, I returned to my seat and was greeted with a raucous round of applause.

I think most of the passengers were still in shock.

Bree stared at me with a look of relief on her face. "That was... impressive. What was it that you do for a living again?"

I flashed her a cocksure grin.

It wasn't all sunshine and roses. An angry woman stormed to me with a scowl on her face. "You could have gotten us all killed! Did you stop to think for one second about the lives you put in jeopardy? Whatever that terrorist had in that spray bottle could be circulating through the cabin now. We might all be dead!"

I just smiled at her.

Somebody in the back shouted, "Shut up and sit down!"

The cabin filled with boos.

4

The angry woman finally returned to her seat. To my surprise, we kept flying to Nice.

We had already passed the halfway point by the time the terrorists attacked, and from a fuel standpoint, it made more sense to continue the journey.

The plane was quarantined upon landing. We sat on the tarmac for hours while the authorities figured out how to handle the situation. The French version of the FBI, the DST, took over.

The instant we landed, a flurry of texts dinged on my phone. They all flooded in now that I had cell-service again. The first message was from Aria:

[Hey, I hope you haven't left yet.]

It was time stamped 10 hours ago.

I cringed.

The second text read: [Don't kill me, but I have to go back to New York. I just got booked on a massive campaign with huge clients. So if you haven't left yet, don't. I'm flying back to New York in an hour. I am so sorry. I promise, I will make it up to you].

A text, time-stamped a few moments, later read: [I haven't heard back from you. I hope you're not on the plane yet, :( ].

The text after that read: [I guess you're already in the air. Don't hate me. Call me when you land. I'm so sorry. :( ].

It was followed by several heart emojis.

A frown tensed my face, and a range of emotions swirled within me. Anger and disappointment mixed, forming a cocktail of irritation.

I took a deep breath and tried to let it go.

Aria had an opportunity and she took it. I wasn't going to begrudge her that. It was part of being a model. I assumed she was telling me the truth about the job, but anything was possible? Besides, I couldn't be too mad... I would never have met Bree otherwise. *I also wouldn't have been involved in a hijacking situation, but considering the way things turned out, it was a small price to pay.*

"Bad news?" Bree asked.

My frustration was apparent. "Change of plans. The person I was meeting in Monaco is no longer *in* Monaco."

"I'm sorry," she said. "Don't worry. I'm sure you'll have a good time no matter what. After a flight like this, things can only get better, right?"

"I like your attitude."

"No reason to dwell on the negative." She smiled.

I was getting used to her smile.

The authorities created a positive pressure airlock around the main entry door—a clear plastic bubble with a fan that pumped in air. It would theoretically keep pathogens from escaping.

A guy in a hazmat suit boarded the plane. The bloated yellow suit covered him from head to toe, and he wore a helmet with a wide clear facemask. He looked like a spaceman that would be at home traipsing around some alien world. He took possession of the nasal spray and put it into an airtight container that had clear side-walls and gloved portals.

He ran a series of tests, and after 30 minutes determined that the solution inside the nasal spray was, in fact, *saline*.

Harmless salt water.

We all breathed a collective sigh of relief as word spread throughout the cabin.

The passengers were more than ready to get off the plane. There were a lot of frazzled nerves that needed to be soothed. I imagined that the first stop for many travelers would be the airport bar.

The flight attendant's voice crackled over the intercom. "I'm told that we will be allowed to deplane shortly. Please remain calm and stay in your seats until that time."

There were groans and complaints. The passengers were getting cranky and hungry.

The flight attendants did their best to keep serving snacks

and beverages, but the aircraft needed to be resupplied.

Once the plane was officially declared safe, the DST agents removed the terrorists and took them into custody. The body of the Air Marshal was removed, and finally we were allowed to deplane. We had to go through customs and were debriefed by the DST. I ended up in an interrogation room for hours, going over every detail of the incident with the agents.

I recounted the details several times. The tiny room was hot, and I was hungry and tired. I stared at the agents, bleary-eyed, as they asked me the same questions in multiple ways, looking to see if my answers ever changed.

It seemed like they were never going to release me. "How many times do you want me to tell you the same thing?"

"We are just trying to be thorough," the lead investigator said with a thick French accent.

He wore a suit and tie and had dark hair, dark eyes, and a narrow face. He didn't smile, or seem appreciative in any way. You'd have thought I was the bad guy. "What is your business in France?"

I thought it would be a good idea to leave out the part about the assassination. "I'm traveling to Monaco."

"For what purpose?"

I smiled. "Why does anyone go to Monaco?"

He frowned at me. "Where will you be staying?"

I shrugged. "How is any of this relevant?" I asked, my voice thick with frustration. "There were two terrorists on board the plane. I stopped them."

"How did you acquire the weapon?"

"Like I told you, the weapon belonged to the Air Marshal. The terrorist took it. I took it from him. By the way, a *thank you* would be nice. That could have gone so many ways of wrong."

"Yes, it could have."

Another agent entered the room and whispered something into the lead investigator's ear. His demeanor changed. "Why didn't you tell me you were Bree Taylor's bodyguard?"

I tried to hide the confusion that crinkled on my face. I stammered, then lied, "I try to keep that information low profile."

"Okay. You are free to go. Please keep us informed of your whereabouts, and do not leave the country without contacting us first. We may have additional questions."

I pushed away from the table and stood up, shook the man's hand, and stepped into the hallway where another agent handed me my carry-on bag.

I was totally shocked to see Bree waiting for me. "What are you still doing here?"

She smiled. "I couldn't leave without thanking you for what you did. You saved all of us." She whispered in my ear, "Plus, I told them you were my bodyguard, and they had to let you go because I needed to be someplace."

"Bodyguard? I like the sound of that." I would definitely guard her body well.

"It's not technically a lie," she said. "I do feel safer with you around. And you did save my life." Her bright eyes glimmered at me. "Come on. You can ride with me. You're traveling to Monaco, right?"

5

Before we could leave, we met with someone from the U.S. State Department and gave another account of the incident. This interview went smoother now that I was with Bree.

Afterward, a private helicopter took us from Nice to Monaco.

The rotor blades pattered overhead, and we lifted from the tarmac. We flew through the night sky, and I wasn't able to see much of the French countryside. The lights of Monaco flickered on the horizon, and within 10 minutes we were landing on a helipad.

"Where are you staying?" Bree asked.

I shrugged. "I don't know. I was going to stay with a friend, but she bailed back to New York. I don't even know what I'm doing here."

Bree smiled. "It's settled. You'll stay with me."

Someone got the door, and we climbed out of the helicopter.

We were shuffled into a limousine, and our baggage was tossed into the trunk. A moment later, the driver climbed behind the wheel and pulled the door shut. "Where to, Ma'am?"

"The harbor," Bree replied.

The driver whisked us across the luxurious city to the marina. It was packed with luxury yachts and spectacular sailboats. There were a few smaller boats, and when I say small, I mean 25 footers. Most of the boats were between 65 and 200 feet—floating palaces of the mega-rich.

I strolled with Bree down the dock while the driver attended to our bags. We passed several shipboard parties along the way.

The whole city had a festive atmosphere.

"The film festival," Bree said. "At Cannes. It's not far from here. There are a lot of parties this time of year, plus there is the Grand Prix in Monaco at the end. We should go."

"To the festival, or to the Grand Prix?"

"Both. I've got a film screening in the festival. And I know Armond Lémieux. He drives for Ferrari. He always gets me free tickets." She grabbed my arm and pulled herself close. Her steamy breath hit my ear as she whispered, "I think he's got a thing for me. But I'm not interested."

Who wouldn't have a thing for her?

"Who do you have a thing for?" I had to ask.

She pretended to think about it for a moment. "I don't know," she said, coyly. "I just met this guy, he's pretty handy to have around in a pinch."

"Is he good in hijacking situations?"

"Exceptional," she said with a smile. Her hand slid down my forearm and took my hand as we strolled down the dock. We stopped in front of a spectacular boat where a party was in full swing.

"This is it," Bree said.

"This is your boat?" I said, my eyes taking in the massive mega-yacht. "Impressive."

"Now you know why my financial manager wants me to curtail my spending. This, along with some bad investments, has got me looking forward to my next payday." She put her finger to her full lips. "But don't tell anyone."

"*Silver Screams*?" I asked, noting the name of the boat.

"I got my start in B-movie horror films. Look where it took me," she said, gesturing to the floating palace. "Never forget where you came from."

We crossed the gangway to the large aft deck and joined the party. It was full of slick LA types. Guys in suits wearing sunglasses at night and models wearing skimpy dresses that sparkled in the light. Pop music pumped through speakers, and staff served cocktails and hors d'oeuvres.

"I'll introduce you," she said.

A flamboyant man in a *Zangari* suit, a *Piere Léon* cotton broadcloth shirt, and matching pocket square approached with his arms outstretched. He had dark hair and perfect features. There wasn't a hair out of place on his head. "Bree, my darling! Thank God you're okay. I was worried sick about you!"

The two embraced.

"Joel, I'd like you to meet Tyson Wild. Tyson, this is my agent Joel Järvi."

We shook hands.

"So, you're the guy?" Joel asked. He looked to Bree for confirmation. "This is him, right? Your superhero?"

Bree laughed.

Joel's eyes met mine. "I am forever indebted to you. You saved the life of my best client. She makes me a lot of money," he said in singsong to the side. "It's just an amazing story. I'm gonna have you two booked on every talk show. It will be great publicity."

The wheels of possibility spun behind his eyes. "I'll bet I can get you a book deal. Do you have an agent?"

"No," I said, putting my hands up, trying to put the brakes on. "Book deals, talk shows... not really my thing."

Joel's eyes flicked to Bree. "Oh, so this one is shy?"

He looked back to me. "We'll fix that. Especially when you see the paycheck I can get you."

I looked at him, skeptically.

"I'm serious. I'm not bullshitting you. This isn't drunk Hollywood talk. I might be a little inebriated, but believe me, I never bullshit when I talk money." His eyes danced to Bree again. "Tell him."

"He's the real deal."

"How long are you in town for?" Joel asked.

I shrugged.

"Good. We'll chat more about this later. I'll have a contract drafted that you can look over tomorrow. Trust me, you won't find better representation."

"I'll think about it," I said, still uncertain.

"Hard to get? I like it."

Joel kissed Bree on the cheek. "So glad you're safe. We'll talk soon." He turned to me. "I want to hear all about it. Every detail."

"Not much to tell," I said.

"He's being modest," Bree said.

"Modesty will get you nowhere. Own it," he said with a grin.

"If you'll excuse me, I'm going to go close a deal." His eyes were fixed on a producer across the boat. Joel made a beeline for his next target.

"Joel's a really good guy," Bree said. "And let me tell you how rare that is to find in Hollywood. I'd think about it if I were you."

"Who's that guy Joel is talking to?" I asked.

"That's Nails. I don't know what his real name is. He finances a lot of bigger independent films."

Nails had a gorgeous aspiring actress on either arm.

"If you're looking to invest in film, you'll get an open invite to just about every party in town," Bree said, dryly.

"Can I get you something to drink?" a waiter asked as he strolled by.

"I'll take a glass of Chardonnay," Bree said.

"Whiskey, rocks," I added.

"Coming right up."

I glanced around the boat, taking in the crowd. I saw several familiar faces. "Is that...?" I asked, motioning across the deck.

"Ugh. Yes," Bree said with an eye roll.

"Bad blood?"

"Long story." She paused for a moment, then decided to answer. "I briefly dated the lead singer of his band. It was about that time he decided to embark on a solo career, so Zazzle blames me. Thinks I instigated it. You know. Yoko Ono syndrome." Her face scrunched up. "Who invited him here, anyway?"

"You always let people party on your boat while you're away?"

"I had Joel arrange it. I planned on being in town a lot sooner. But I wouldn't be here at all if it weren't for you." There was that bright smile again.

It was no wonder the whole world loved this woman.

The waiter returned with the drinks. Bree and I toasted.

"To life," she said.

"To life," I replied.

We clinked glasses, and I took a sip of my whiskey. It was

smooth and warmed my belly. After the day I'd had, it was a welcomed indulgence. By this point, I had been rolling on 36 hours without sleep and was feeling a little punchy.

"You're not going to quit early on me, are you?" Bree said, noticing my droopy eyes.

"Mama didn't raise no quitter."

"Good. Because I like to work hard and play hard." Her blue eyes pierced into me again. Something about the way she said *hard* was very alluring.

There was no doubt about it. This girl was more than just flirting with me. If I played my cards right, I was probably going to have a little bit of fun—if I could stay awake long enough. For Bree, I was pretty sure I could stay awake long enough.

Our magical moment was interrupted by another executive type in a suit. "Bree! I'm so glad you're okay. I heard. It's been all over the news. So crazy!"

The two hugged.

"Liam, I'd like you to meet Tyson. Liam is my financial manager."

"I've heard all about you," I said as I shook the man's hand.

Liam Gordon was tall and skinny with sandy blonde hair and a baby face. His suit was expensive. So were his Italian shoes.

"Good things, I hope," Liam said with an insincere smile.

"I told him you put me on a budget," Bree said.

Liam laughed. "Putting her on a budget is like trying to reel in Congress when it comes to spending."

I chuckled.

"Where's Elena?" Bree asked.

He pointed across the deck to a striking brunette in a little black cocktail dress that attempted to hide nothing. Like most of the women on this boat, she was easy on the eyes.

Liam patted my shoulder. "Nice to meet you."

He strolled across the deck and greeted other guests.

"Two of my favorite people," Bree said. "Such a great couple. They seem to make it work, despite all the craziness."

We downed our drinks, and a waiter brought us another round.

"Come on. I'll give you a tour of the boat," Bree said.

She took my hand and pulled me across the deck, into the salon.

The yacht was nothing short of amazing. Sleek lines and elegant appointments. The finest Italian furniture, and leather wall panels, high ceilings, wood with mother-of-pearl accents, and silk carpets. The main deck salon opened to a dining area and a bar. The lounge area had a luxurious sofa and a large flatscreen display was mounted on a retractable stand. The guest suites were on the lower deck with a stunning full beam master cabin, complete with a queen berth, flat screen TV, and en suite.

Forward of the master was the VIP guest suite with a full birth and private en suite. There were three more guest quarters with stacked bunks that shared two en suites that also served as day heads.

There was a massage room, a work out room, a sauna, several lounge areas, and multiple bars.

It made JD's boat look like a hunk of junk.

"163', built by Ultramarine. Designed by Adimari. Five cabins that sleep 12, +9 crew. Two MTU engines for a total of 8000 kW and a top speed of 30 knots. It has a main deck, sundeck, and a Jacuzzi on the forward bow."

"I don't even want to ask how much this cost."

"According to Liam, too much." She laughed, then sighed.

Continuing the tour, we rounded the corner and were greeted by a woman holding a knife.

She had crazed eyes.

Bree instantly recoiled, taking shelter behind me.

"Carolyn, what are you doing here?" Bree asked, her voice trembling. "This is private property, you're trespassing! You need to leave now!"

"Friend of yours?" I muttered dryly to Bree.

6

"Just take it easy, and put down the knife," I said in a soothing voice.

Carolyn glanced to the large kitchen knife that was in her hand, glimmering in the light. "Oh. I found this on the deck. I didn't want anybody to step on it and get hurt. I was bringing it back to the galley."

She held the knife out to me.

"Just set it on the deck," I said, regarding her with caution.

Bree trembled behind me.

Carolyn complied with my request. She knelt down and placed the knife on the deck.

"Take a few steps back," I commanded.

"Um, okay." She had a confused look on her face, like it was no big deal that she was holding a knife, and why the hell were we so freaked out?

When she stepped away, I scooped the knife up. "I think it's time for you to leave."

Carolyn's face twisted, confused. "But I thought you wanted me here?"

"Why would you think that, Carolyn?" Bree asked. "I have a restraining order against you. You're not supposed to come within 100 feet of me."

"I know. But that's in the United States."

"So? You're trespassing on my boat," Bree said, sternly.

"Well, I just thought... I was concerned. There was this little voice in the back of my head that said Bree's in trouble. She needs your help. And I knew you were going to be in Monaco. I saw it on the news. And—"

"I appreciate your concern, Carolyn," Bree said. "But it's time for you to go."

"Are you sure you're okay?"

"I'm fine," Bree said with a clenched jaw. Her face was red. The veins in her neck pulsed.

"I just have this terrible feeling..."

I took Carolyn's arm and escorted her down the corridor. "Come on. Party's over."

I walked her to the aft deck and across the gangway. I helped her onto the dock.

She looked distraught—her face crinkled with worry.

"Are you going to leave her alone, or do I need to call the police?" I asked.

She stammered, "No. That won't be necessary. I'll go. Will you just make sure she's okay?"

"She'll be fine. I'll see to it."

I stepped back onto the gangway of *Silver Screams* and watched Carolyn skulk away. Her body slumped, and her chest deflated like a balloon. She kept looking back over her shoulder at me with a pathetic gaze.

Once she was gone, I returned to the salon and found Bree. She was sitting on the sofa, her hands trembling. She had switched from Chardonnay to whiskey to soothe her nerves.

"Are you okay?" I asked as I set the kitchen knife on the coffee table and took a seat beside her.

I put my arm around her and she leaned into my shoulder.

"Yeah, I'm just a little freaked out."

"Who was that?"

"She's this crazy stalker of mine. She shows up everywhere. She even got inside my home once. I always figured she was relatively harmless, but when I saw her with that knife, I thought this was it—I survived the hijacking just to get killed by some crazed fan."

"Nothing's going to happen to you as long as you're with me," I said.

Bree put a hand on my chest as she rested her head on my shoulder. "That's why I'm going to keep you around."

"You want me to call the police?"

"Is she gone?"

"Yeah. I watched her walk down the dock."

"I don't know how she got aboard?"

"It's a party. People come and go at their leisure."

"It's so weird. She acts like she knows me. She's always trying to give me career advice. She sends letter after letter, telling me which movies I should do, which guys to date. It's crazy. I mean, doesn't she have her own life?"

"It seems you *are* her life."

We sat silent for a long moment. Then Bree took a deep breath. "Well, that's twice you saved me tonight."

"All in a days work," I said, modestly.

"I guess I'll have to put you on the payroll," she said with a smirk. She looked up at me with those big blue eyes, and her full lips inched closer to mine.

I was not about to pass this opportunity up.

Our lips collided, and our tongues danced. The sweet smell of her shampoo filled my nostrils. Bombs burst in the air, and the earth rumbled. I don't know if the kiss was THAT good, or if I was just starstruck?

Butterflies flitted in my stomach. Her lips were pillowy soft, and I wouldn't mind if this line of action continued all night.

We made out on the couch. With Bree in my arms, it was easy to forget there was a party going on.

"Get a room!" a drunk voice slurred.

Bree and I broke from our embrace.

"Fuck off, Zazzle!" Bree barked.

He swayed over us with a bottle of whiskey dangling from a skinny tattooed forearm. Studded bracelets lined his wrists, and the veins popped out of his lanky arms. Long stringy black hair concealed a narrow face and bloodshot eyes, lined with black liner. He wore a sleeveless denim vest, and leather pants. "Don't you have careers to ruin? Bands to break up?"

"I didn't break up your band," Bree protested. "Finn was planning a solo project long before we started dating."

"For your information, you two weren't dating. He was just fucking you."

Bree's eyes narrowed at him. "Eat me."

"No thanks." Zazzle leaned toward me. "You might want to rubber up if you tap this one. She's been around."

"You're such an asshole," Bree muttered under her breath.

My jaw clenched tight, and my fingers balled into fists. I just met Bree, but I didn't appreciate this scumbag talking about her that way.

I launched to my feet and got in the rockstar's face. I didn't care who he was. "Apologize!"

He scoffed. "For what?"

"Apologize to the lady," I demanded.

"Dude, I will kick your fucking teeth in."

I grabbed his long skinny hair and yanked it toward the deck. He hunched over and his neck bent down.

He swung the bottle of whiskey at me that was dangling from his left hand.

I blocked the blow and stripped the bottle and twisted a fistful of his hair. I gripped the neck of the whiskey bottle, ready to smash it against his face. "Apologize to the lady before things get ugly."

He whimpered, "I'm sorry."

I let his hair go, and he stood up and slung the greasy locks aside. "Jesus Christ, man. Ease up!"

He tried to compose himself. He glanced around to see if anyone had seen the incident, then he strutted away like nothing had happened.

I took a seat beside Bree and set the bottle of whiskey on the glass coffee table. "Are you always surrounded by this much drama?"

"Hollywood is worse than high school." She leaned in and kissed me on the cheek. "Thank you for defending my honor."

"His behavior was uncalled for."

"I'm not a slut, I swear." She looked at me with those adorable blue eyes that were filled with concern.

I chuckled. "I didn't think you were. You think I'm going to give what that guy says any merit?"

She shrugged, meekly. "So, if I jump your bones tonight, you won't think less of me?"

7

"Excuse me, but I need to borrow her for a minute," Joel said.

He pulled Bree off the sofa and escorted her across the salon to speak with a famous director.

I stood up from the couch and walked deeper into the salon where it opened into a formal dining area, bar, and home theater. I ordered another whiskey on the rocks, and the bartender refreshed my glass.

Before I could take the first sip, another sultry movie star slinked next to me at the bar. She was a gorgeous brunette, Savannah Skye. I recognized her from a number of movies. It was surprising how normal this was all beginning to seem.

"So, you're the talk of the town right now," Savannah said.

"Really?" I said, feigning modesty.

"Bree sure seems to be smitten," she said in a smug tone.

"She's a nice girl."

I could tell by the look on Savannah's face that she didn't share the same opinion. "That bitch stole a role from me. She slept with David Cameron to get a role in *UltraMega*."

Bree glanced over to us, and Savannah smiled and waved. She muttered under her breath. "I hope that bitch falls overboard and drowns. Then gets eaten by sharks."

I arched an astonished eyebrow. "Tell me how you really feel?"

Her eyes smoldered at me. She pressed her enticing body against mine, and in a breathy voice that slipped from her velvety lips she said, "I feel like I want to fuck you, just to piss her off."

It certainly was quite the offer. One that I normally wouldn't decline. "Thanks, but I'll pass."

Her seductive grin turned into a scowl. Savannah twisted her shoulder away and stormed off with a huff.

I laughed to myself. Bree was right, this is way worse than high school ever thought about being.

It was interesting to see that these big celebrities were more insecure than just about anybody I'd ever met. They traded on their looks and charisma, and when that faded, their careers were over. A few lucky ones had longevity, but most became has-beens within a matter of years. It seemed if you had any amount of success, jealousy followed. Everybody waited in the wings, ready to tear you down at a moment's notice. It sounded like a life that I didn't want any part of. Though I had to admit, being surrounded by backstabbing, conniving lowlifes was probably better than being surrounded by assassins. As treacherous as Hollywood could be, it was nothing compared to the life of a clandestine agent.

Bree returned a few minutes later and greeted me at the bar. I leaned with my elbows against the counter, watching all the people.

"I see you met Savannah," she said.

"Interesting girl. Not a fan of yours."

"I'm sure she told you something nasty about me."

"Indeed."

"It's hard to make real friends in this business."

"I've noticed."

"If you get involved with it, don't let it change you," she cautioned.

"Trust me, I've been in way more treacherous situations than the entertainment industry."

"I don't doubt that."

Her eyes caught sight of someone across the salon, and a sour look curdled on her face. "Excuse me just a minute. I promise after this, I'm all yours."

Bree stormed to a man who wore a white linen suit, royal blue shirt, and a matching pocket square. His skin was so tanned he looked like he lived on the beach 24/7. His brown hair had blonde highlights. He looked like something out of an 80s pop music video.

Bree pulled him aside, and the two had an intense conversation in a hushed tone. She returned a moment later, and the man disappeared into the crowd.

"What was that about?" I asked.

"Ugh. Vincent Villeneuve. Don't get me started."

"You haven't finished giving me the tour of your boat," I said.

"We keep getting interrupted. I'm sorry."

She grabbed my hand with a flirty smile and pulled me to the lower deck. She showed me the master suite. It was impressive. A queen-size berth on a riser with a storage compartment underneath. End tables on either side with fixed lamps. Glossy wood-paneled walls, recessed lighting, surround-sound stereo system, flat-screen display, a mini-bar, and plush carpeting.

It looked more like a luxury hotel room than a master suite on a boat. My jaw dropped, and my eyes widened as I took in a panoramic view of the suite. "This is... nice."

My eyes caught sight of a Cubist piece of art on the bulkhead. "Is that a...?"

"Picasso?" She nodded and pulled me close. "I didn't bring you down here to talk."

Our lips were inches apart. My heart skipped a few beats as she drew near. Her piercing blue eyes stared into me, and I felt like I was back in high school again and this was my first kiss—even though we'd just made out on the couch.

She planted her full lips on mine, and I put my hand on the small of her back and pulled her close.

The whole thing was surreal.

Her warm body pressed against mine, and my blood rushed south. I devoured her pillowy soft lips. My hands traced the supple curves of her body as we embraced.

I forgot all about the hijacking, my lack of sleep, the Picasso on the wall, the crazy drama on the boat, and lost myself in the moment.

It was like a dream.

She slipped out of her sundress, and the fabric slid down her body and pooled around her ankles. I caught a glimpse of something nobody saw on the silver screen.

My eyes drank in her magnificent form. My God, she was perfect. Her perky breasts, her toned abs, her elegant thighs. She knew what she'd been gifted with, and her eyes sparkled as she watched me soak up the moment.

But I wanted to do more than just look.

We fell onto the bed and tumbled around in the sheets. Our bodies collided with passion. When it was all said and done with, we both had big smiles on our faces.

I collapsed beside her, drenched in sweat, exhausted. I lay there in a blissful state, holding a beautiful movie star in my arms.

It was unreal, and I fully expected to wake up in the morning to discover it was all a fantasy.

I didn't know where this was going, and at that point it didn't really matter. This could have been a one-night thing? Maybe it was a week-long tryst? Maybe it was the start of something more?

I couldn't really imagine that a movie star like her would be interested in someone like me for the long-term, but I was all about exploring the opportunities that life presented.

And this was a hell of an opportunity.

I lay there so relaxed, I could barely keep my eyes open, and promptly crashed out. I slept like a rock, despite the muffled sounds of the party that filtered into the suite.

When I woke up in the morning, I didn't know where the hell I was. I peeled my eyes open and glanced around the master stateroom, and the dream-like memories of last night came flooding back.

My hand felt the sheets beside me—they were cold and empty.

Bree was gone.

8

I strolled up to the main deck, looking for Bree. In the main dining area, a breakfast spread had been elegantly presented—juice, donuts, croissants, silver hot trays with eggs, bacon, and hash browns.

I grabbed a cup of coffee, dished up a plate, and took a seat.

A few moments later, the chef emerged from the galley. "Is there anything else I can get for you?"

"No, thank you. This is great. Do you know where Bree is?"

The chef shrugged. "I haven't seen her yet this morning. I can check with the other staff. But there are only a few of us right now."

The cook disappeared below deck and returned a few moments later to tell me that no one had seen her this morning.

I finished breakfast, then strolled around the ship, taking in the magnificent vessel. I could certainly get used to a life like this, but I couldn't imagine how much cash it would take to sustain it?

There were dozens of mega-yachts in the marina. This wasn't the biggest. What the hell did these people do for a living?

It was a beautiful day. There was a cool breeze off the water, and gulls squawked in the air. The gentle waves lapped against the hull. It was 64°, and not a cloud in the sky.

I didn't have Bree's phone number, but I figured one of the staff members might. I found the cook, and he gave me the number, but she didn't answer.

I thought Bree might have left early for a meeting with her agent, or had some errands to run? The daily life of a celebrity was not something I was familiar with. What did they do when they weren't making movies?

I left a note in the master suite with my phone number in case Bree returned while I was out. I decided to stroll around Monaco and take in the sights.

There were high-end shopping boutiques and supercars on every corner. I saw the casino and knew I was going to hit the tables before the end of my trip. The city was nothing short of opulent, and the Belle Époque architecture was amazing, juxtaposed against sleek, modernist structures.

I strolled down to the man-made beach with imported sand and people-watched. String bikinis struggled to contain toned bodies. Taut fabric pressed against firm assets. It was a visual feast.

After soaking in the sights, I walked to a coffee shop and got a cup of java. I took a seat at a table on the sidewalk and enjoyed the pleasant morning breeze. The warm amber sun cast long shadows, slipping through alleyways, peering over rooftops. It was quiet, and the city was just beginning to stir.

I called JD, not very mindful of the time difference between Monaco and Coconut Key.

"Do you know what time it is?" JD grumbled.

"Were you asleep?"

"No."

"Then no harm, no foul."

I told him about my adventure on the plane, and my encounter with Bree Taylor.

"You're pulling my leg," JD said.

"Nope. Hand to God, I'm telling you the truth."

"Lucky bastard."

"What can I say? The travel gods smiled upon me."

"What happened to Aria?"

I sighed. "She went back to New York. She was gone before I got here."

"Well, sounds like everything worked out, anyway."

"How's Scarlett?"

"I've got her on the straight and narrow, I think. She's got another court date next month. With any luck we can get this thing dismissed," JD said. "But I'm not letting her out of my sight."

"Alright, just checking in. I'll catch up with you later."

"Pics or it didn't happen," JD added.

I chuckled and realized I didn't have any photos of myself with Bree. No one would believe the story. I'm sure JD regarded it with a healthy dose of skepticism.

"By the way, I'm going to look at a few new boats tomorrow."

"Man, you'd love this place. You would not believe some of the yachts in the harbor. Unreal. You'd die if you saw Bree's boat."

"Rub it in, why don't you?" Jack grumbled. Then he tried to sound pathetic, "I see how it is. Leave your best friend behind while you go gallivanting around with movie stars and the mega-rich."

"I'm having a miserable time," I lied. "Does that make you feel better?"

JD scoffed. "Yeah, right. Don't have too much fun, you little bastard."

I laughed again and told JD I'd talk to him later. He made me promise to give him detailed situation reports.

I'd been gone several hours, and I hadn't heard anything from the movie star. I was beginning to worry I had gotten ditched. Again. First, my on-again, off-again model girlfriend runs out on me, now the movie star...?

I guess there are worse things in life.

Maybe Bree was trying to get rid of me?

I walked back to the harbor and found my way to the *Silver*

Screams. There were several uniformed police officers waiting for me.

They wore white shirts and royal blue pants with a red stripe down the side. Their duty hats were royal blue with a matching red band. A plainclothes detective stood among them.

By the look on their faces, they weren't here for a party.

"I am Inspector Jean-Pierre Géroux," he said in English with a thick French accent. "Monsieur Wild, I presume?"

9

The inspector was holding the note I had left for Bree. I assumed that's how he knew my name.

He had dark hair, a narrow face, and a large nose that overhung a thick mustache. His suit looked like it had seen plenty of days on the job.

"What's going on?" I asked.

"We'd like to ask you a few questions," the inspector said.

"Has something happened?"

There was a long pause.

"Where were you last night?"

I didn't like the direction this was going. "I was here. I woke up this morning, had breakfast, then walked to town. You mind telling me what's going on?"

"Were you with Miss Taylor last night?"

"Yes."

"When was the last time you saw her?"

"Has something happened to her?" My throat tightened.

Géroux hesitated for a moment. "Miss Taylor is deceased."

His words felt like a punch to the gut. The news left me breathless. My throat grew dry and tight, and I barely choked out, "How?"

"When was the last time you saw her?"

"Last night, around midnight, I guess."

"Where?"

"In the master stateroom."

"Were you to... involved?"

I stammered, "You could say so."

"Perhaps we should finish this conversation down at the station?"

My eyes narrowed at him. "Are you arresting me?"

"I'm merely trying to ascertain what happened."

"You don't seriously consider me a suspect, do you?"

"I never said this was a homicide."

"You wouldn't be taking me to the station otherwise."

Géroux paused. "I must consider all options. As I said, I believe this conversation would be more comfortable at the station."

"Do I have a choice?"

He shook his head.

I knew better than to talk to cops, but I wasn't familiar with Monegasque law, which was essentially derived from the French Code.

I spent several hours in a tiny interrogation room at the station, going over the same questions with Inspector Géroux. I was finally able to ascertain that Bree's body had been found floating in the ocean. She had bruises on her body and lacerations about her head. It was thought she'd been struck and pushed overboard.

The high profile nature of the case ramped up the desire for a speedy resolution. I just hoped that I wasn't going to be the fall guy.

"Isn't there any surveillance footage from the harbor?" I asked.

"Unfortunately, no. Several cameras have been damaged, and the system is awaiting repair."

"Have you interviewed potential witnesses? The neighboring boats? Surely somebody saw something?"

"I know how to do my job, Mr. Wild," Géroux said, sharply.

"I want a lawyer. And don't I get a phone call?" I asked.

Inspector Géroux nodded to one of the uniformed officers. He escorted me out of the interrogation room and down the hall to a phone. I made a collect international call to JD's landline and prayed that he would answer.

When the operator asked if he would accept the charges, JD knew this wasn't going to be a social call. "What kind of trouble are you in?" "It's not good. I need you to call the Embassy and find me a lawyer."

"Who did you kill?" JD asked in jest.

"Not funny."

"Oh, shit," JD muttered, knowingly. "Really?"

I filled him in on the situation.

"Okay. I'm on it," JD said. "I'll make some calls, then I guess I'll hop on a plane."

"No. You need to stay there and look after Scarlett."

"I'll get Madison to look after her. She could use a little time with a positive female role model."

"I appreciate you, brother," I said.

I hung up the phone and was escorted to a holding cell. I hadn't been officially charged with anything yet, and I think they were just keeping me around until they had a better idea of what happened.

I was certainly a flight risk.

Everything about the city was luxurious, and the jail was no exception. It was immaculate. I had never seen a cleaner facility. It was nicer than some hotels I had stayed in. The paint was fresh, the bunk mattress was comfortable, and the place didn't smell like a sewer pit.

Monaco is one of the safest places on earth. There are over 500 police officers, and with a total population of less than 40,000, the principality has the highest per capita law enforcement of any place on the planet. There are security cameras everywhere, and though there is still crime, it's not like the jail is overflowing with criminals.

I had the cell all to myself, and despite the minimalist nature of my accommodations, I had a decent night's sleep.

To my surprise, the next morning I was released.

"I'm sorry for the inconvenience," Inspector Géroux said as he opened my cell.

I flashed him a curious look.

A man in a suit standing next to him shook my hand and introduced himself as Francois Lévêque, my advocate.

His *Alesini Couture* double-breasted suit was dark gray with pinstripes and peak lapels. A lavender shirt and dark tie coordinated with a patterned pocket square. A *Brunetti* watch adorned his wrist, and a *Capello* leather attaché hung from his fingers. The outfit, including the *A. Donati* leather cap-toed shoes, probably cost $10,000. My guess was that the hip, thirty-something lawyer didn't come cheap.

He took my arm and pulled me down the corridor, trying to get me out of the jail as quickly as possible.

I was a little befuddled. Don't get me wrong, I was happy to be out of that cell, but I didn't like being left in the dark. "Have they got another suspect in custody?"

"The coroner has determined the death to be of an accidental nature," Francois said. "Drowning. Miss Taylor had a considerable amount of alcohol in her system, mixed with a narcotic."

"A narcotic?" I hadn't seen her take any pills, but I wasn't with her every second of the evening either.

"It is believed that she fell overboard, sustained injuries about the head during the fall, rendering her unconscious. Then she drowned."

It would take a while for me to process the information. I was still having a hard time believing Bree was dead.

My attorney escorted me through the facility, and my belongings were returned at the exit-processing station. There were dozens of texts and missed calls on my phone. I'd get to them later.

I was buzzed through a secure door and stepped into the waiting area where I saw JD. He'd taken the evening flight and just gotten into Monaco half an hour ago.

He greeted me with a big smile. "I let you out of my sight for two days, and this is what happens?"

He gave me a big hug.

"I owe you one," I said.

"Mr. Donovan has taken care of my fee," François said. "I will handle all questions when we step outside. Do not say a word." His stern eyes blazed into me.

François motioned toward the door, and we exited.

A horde of reporters swarmed the jail. The brilliant flashes from hundreds of cameras spotted my eyes as we stepped outside. Questions were hurled at me like fastballs, some in English, some in French.

"Did you kill her?"

"Were you lovers?"

"Are you still a person of interest?"

I did my best to shelter my face as François led us through the horde of vultures.

"Miss Taylor's death has been ruled accidental," François said. "My client is innocent of any and all wrongdoing."

At the curb, we stepped into a limo that was waiting for us. We left the screeching reporters behind as we zipped through the city.

I knew my picture was going to be on the cover of every paper across the globe. I wasn't thrilled about the exposure. There were people out there that wanted me dead, and now they knew exactly where I was.

"Can you get a copy of the official autopsy report?" I asked.

"Yes, it is a matter of public record," François said.

"I'd like to see it."

"If I were you, I would go home. Try to go about your life as best you can. There are no travel restrictions on your visa. It would be best to leave before someone has a change of heart."

It wasn't bad advice, but I knew I wasn't going to take it. Something didn't sit right with me about the incident, and I was determined to get to the bottom of it.

10

Aria had sent several text messages. She wanted to know if I was okay, and what happened? I'd call her later. I was still a little miffed that she had ditched me.

There were several messages from Isabella, and she was not pleased. Hers was a phone call I needed to return. She wasn't any less angry when I got her on the phone.

"Way to keep a low profile," she said, her voice thick with sarcasm.

"Circumstances beyond my control."

"I sent you to do a job, and we may not get another opportunity," Isabella chided. "You're slipping, Tyson. What were you thinking, getting involved with a celebrity?"

"It sounded appealing at the time."

She wasn't amused.

"I need you to do me a favor," I said.

"Your ability to call in favors is a little weak right now."

"I'll make it up to you."

Isabella scoffed. "I've heard that one before. Let me give you a piece of advice. Stop digging—the hole you're in is deep enough."

I ignored her. "Can you get all the text messages that were sent to and from Bree Taylor's phone?"

There was a long silence.

Isabella was my point person at Cobra Company—a clandestine organization made up of former spooks and spec-war operators that worked on a contract basis, doing all the dirty deeds that the intelligence community didn't want to be held accountable for. There was no phone they couldn't tap. No computer system they couldn't hack into. No code they couldn't crack. And they didn't have to play by the rules.

Isabella finally sighed, "Fine. Give me the number."

I did.

"Don't bother looking for Cartwright," Isabella grumbled. "He's long gone by now."

"I figured."

She hung up before I finished speaking.

We returned to Port Hercule. My bag was still aboard the *Silver Screams*. I had an unsettled feeling in my stomach as I walked down the dock toward Bree's yacht.

"You've got a lot of nerve coming back here," Liam said as I stepped aboard.

His eyes were filled with pure hatred, and the muscles in his jaw flexed. Rage and sadness swirled within him. The veins in his neck bulged.

"I don't know if you've heard the news, but Bree's death was ruled an accident," I said, though I didn't believe it.

Liam's eyes narrowed at me. "I can tell you, it wasn't an accident." His face flushed. "You need to leave."

"I didn't kill her. And what makes you so sure it wasn't an accident?" He knew Bree far better than I did, and I wanted to get his take on the incident.

"Why are you here?" he said, disregarding my question.

"I need my bag."

We stared each other down for a long moment.

"Get your things, and get out!" he said through gritted teeth.

There were a few other people in the salon that I didn't recognize. I went below deck and into the master stateroom. I took a moment to breathe in the room. The subtle traces of Bree's perfume still lingered in the air. I thought about how much fun we had in this room, and how somber things were now. Her death left a gaping hole in many people's lives. I felt it, and I had only known her for a day.

I grabbed my roller bag and returned to the main deck. "Has anybody talked to the neighboring boat owners?"

Liam clenched his jaw. "What part of *leave* did you not understand?"

"Look, I'm just as distraught as you are."

"I doubt it. You knew her for what, a few hours?"

He was hurt and grieving, and I was the focus of his rage. It was understandable. Everyone close to Bree wanted someone to blame for this. It seemed too bizarre to be an accident, but I guess stranger things have happened.

I left the *Silver Screams* and rejoined JD on the dock.

"That's a hell of a boat," he said, marveling at the magnificent vessel.

"I think you should get one just like it," I said.

"You want to go in halfsies?" he suggested in jest.

I chuckled. "Talk to me when I'm rich and famous."

"You're about to have the famous part. I'm not so sure about the rich." He paused for a moment. "I've got a room at the Hôtel Impérial. It's not the Hermitage, but it will do. I suppose we can catch a flight out in the morning?"

"I think I'm going to stay for a little while."

JD frowned. "I knew you were going to say that."

"I'm not so sure I buy the *drowning* thing."

"Why not? It happens. She gets drunk, pops a few pills..."

"This case got wrapped up a little too neatly, don't you think?"

"You're complaining because you weren't charged with murder?" JD asked, incredulous.

"You know what I mean. Come on... think about it. It's not

good business when celebrities are murdered. Bad for tourism."

JD gave me a skeptical look.

"I'm just saying... If she drowns, it's a tragedy. If she was murdered, that means there's a killer on the loose."

"Okay, Detective. Let's just get a few things out the way. We're in a foreign country. I don't have a gun, do you?"

"No."

"We have no authority here."

"Our authority back in Coconut Key is tenuous at best."

JD made a face at me.

"And when has that ever stopped either of us, anyway?"

"How about we just enjoy a few days on the French Riviera, then go back home?"

"I've got no problem with that. You can enjoy the French Riviera, and I'll search for the person that killed Bree Taylor."

JD's face tensed, clearly annoyed at my stubbornness. "You can't be sure she was murdered."

"I can't be sure she wasn't."

We kept talking as we strolled down the dock.

"You didn't hear anything that night? No commotion? No screams for help? No splashes in the water?"

"Nothing. I hadn't slept in 2 days, my belly was full of whiskey, and I just had some of the best sex of my life."

Jack was green with envy. "Got any leads?"

I shrugged. "A few. Seems there were a lot of people that didn't really like her."

"Why? Was she a raging bitch?"

"That's the thing," I said, perplexed. "She was really nice. Genuine. I think there was a lot of jealousy around her. When you become that successful, people hate you just for breathing. They root for you when you are an underdog, but when you get on top... all they want to do is tear you down."

"I can relate. People have been trying to tear me down for years," he said without a hint of modesty.

I rolled my eyes. Nobody was trying to tear JD down—except, maybe, his ex-wife.

"The way I figure, we've got a week to solve this thing," I said. "Once the film festival is over, most of these Hollywood types are going back to the States."

We went back to the Hôtel Impérial. It wasn't the fanciest place in Monaco, but it was reasonably priced and clean. The rooms were a bit on the small side, but there was WiFi, air conditioning, and a complementary breakfast. It was on Avenue Prince Pierre and was in walking distance to just about everything.

I took a shower, and by the time I got dressed, my stomach was rumbling. There was an Italian restaurant across the street that JD and I decided to try. But we were mobbed when we hit the street.

11

Cameras flashed and reporters shouted more questions. We escaped into the restaurant, and the vultures hovered outside, waiting for our exit.

I could understand why celebrities punched these guys. They stuck camera lenses an inch from my face and were completely shameless in their attempts to snap a marketable picture.

The *D&D* restaurant was a small place on the corner with marble floors, modern mahogany chairs and tables, and pop art on the walls. The maître d' seated us at a table in the back, away from the windows.

The smell of marinara and Italian seasonings wafted through the air. The subtle murmur of conversation filled the restaurant along with the clink of forks against plates. Ice rattled in glasses, and Pellegrino fizzed as a waiter poured the sparkling water at a neighboring table.

A pretty brunette waitress took our order. There were over

30 varieties of pizza and pasta dishes. We decided to split a margarita pizza. Simple and effective.

I kept glancing out to the street. The paparazzi hung around like stray dogs, smoking cigarettes and chatting amongst themselves. The vultures weren't going to give up anytime soon. At least they had the decency to leave us alone while we were in the restaurant.

"Maybe we should just go back home tomorrow," I said.

"Whatever you want to do."

"Maybe Bree *did* drown, and my imagination is running away with me?"

"Trust your gut. Has it ever been wrong?"

I shook my head.

"I know you. When you get these hunches, you're normally spot on."

"I don't know. It's just so hard for me to believe. She was next to me when I went to sleep and gone when I woke up. She died sometime between midnight and 8 AM."

"That's a lot of time. Anything could have happened."

I frowned as I thought about it, racking my brain. I was mad at myself for letting it happen. Her death occurred on my watch, so to speak. I told her I would keep her safe, but I never imagined she'd fall off her own boat and drown. I didn't hear anything that night, and I'm usually a light sleeper.

It was one of those things that would haunt me for the rest of my days if I didn't figure out exactly what happened.

I gobbled down the pizza in a distracted state. The food was excellent and reasonably priced. I'd find out later that it was regarded as some of the best pizza in Monaco.

"Look at it this way," JD said. "We're already here. We both deserve a vacation. Might as well have a little fun in the sun? It will give us a few days to dig around and see if anything turns up. If nothing does, you can put it to rest."

JD knew me well. I didn't have to tell him what was going on in my head. He could see it for himself.

We left the restaurant and were hounded again by the paparazzi. This time I decided not to fight. I stood there and let them take pictures, and I answered questions, keeping my answers short and vague. When they had their fill, they left me alone.

We walked down the street and got a cup of coffee at a sidewalk café. Without the swarm of paparazzi, we could enjoy the breezy afternoon.

JD decided that *cocktail hour* was fast approaching. We left the café and strolled down *Avenue du Port* to a bar that overlooked the marina called *After Hours*. It was a swanky upscale place with a sleek modern interior and LED panels under the bar and in the walls that slowly changed colors over time, giving the bar a different vibe every hour. Pop art paintings of American rock stars lined the walls—Jim Morrison, Keith Richards, Jimi Hendrix, Stevie Ray Vaughn.

It was full of men in designer suits and women in expensive dresses that were barely there. Stiletto heels and toned legs, flawless make up, and styled hair. The clientele wasn't cheap, and neither were the drinks. The staff was friendly, and the ambience was unparalleled.

I leaned against the bar and ordered a whiskey-rocks for JD and I with a beer back. I took in the sights and tried to relax.

The next thing I knew, I was rubbing elbows with a gorgeous brunette. She wore a gold strapless dress. It was hard not to drop my eyes to her sumptuous valley of cleavage that longed to spring free of the taught fabric. Her gravity defying assets were prisoners in desperate need of liberation from the oppressive garment.

The hemline of her dress rode high on her toned olive thighs, barely concealing the holy land. The dress sparkled, and her skin shimmered. She had legs that could start wars, and her sculpted features were classic. Her blue eyes sparkled, and her full pouty lips just begged to be kissed.

She had to be a model.

"I know you," she said with a thick French accent.

I smiled. "I don't think so."

"No, I mean I know your face. You are a someone famous, no?"

"No," I chuckled. "I'm not famous."

Her eyes narrowed at me, and her long black lashes fluttered. "You are here for the festival in Cannes?"

"I'm just here."

"So many celebrities are in Monaco, traveling back and forth. It's very exciting this time of year."

"It is indeed." *Exciting* was an understatement.

"Will you stay for the Grand Prix?"

"Possibly."

"I love watching the races. So fast. So dangerous. My favorite driver is Armond Lémieux. He's so cute." She paused for a moment. "But not as cute as you."

"I'm flattered."

JD leaned around me to get a better look at her. His eyes ogled her shapely form. Her perfect curves were on full display as she leaned against the bar beside me.

"I have it now," she said. "I know who you are."

"You do?"

"You are the suspected killer, no?"

I was getting tired of telling people Bree drowned, especially when I didn't believe it myself. "I'm... I *was* just a friend."

"You two were having an affair, no?"

I didn't say anything.

"That's what they say in the papers, anyway."

"Do you believe everything you read?"

Her eyes brightened with intrigue. She inched even closer and spoke in a sultry voice. "Did you know that the French word for orgasm is *La petite mort*. It means *the little death*."

"I knew that."

"I think I would like you to give me a little death. You are a killer, after all," she said with a lustful glint in her eye.

I smiled. "That's very tempting, but I just spent the night in jail. My friend just died. I'm not in the right headspace."

JD looked at me like I was crazy.

"But I give such great headspace," she said in a pouty voice, followed by a naughty grin.

JD nudged an elbow into my ribs. He muttered in my ear, "If you don't get on that, I will."

12

I was fairly confident that JD could take care of himself. He was a big boy. I left *After Hours* with the stunning brunette in the gold dress. Her name was Katya.

We caught a cab back to her condo, and part of me worried that I might wake up in the morning missing a kidney.

It seemed a little too good to be true. I mean, I had always done reasonably well with women, but in the last few days, I was batting a thousand.

This seemed almost too easy.

Maybe she had a couple guys waiting with lead pipes ready to pummel me and take my wallet?

I almost laughed at the idea—it was a little paranoid. But a healthy dose of paranoia can keep you alive.

During the cab ride, I thought about the older version of me. The one sitting in a nursing home drooling on myself, struggling to remember the good old days. If I lived that long, that old man would probably tell me to live life to the fullest. Enjoy every moment. Take every opportunity. Don't sweat the small stuff, and never turn down a beautiful woman.

My paranoia vanished when I saw her luxury high-rise.

Katya's condo was a two bedroom on the 37th floor of the *Parthenon Towers.* It must have cost a small fortune. It was around 2500 ft.^{2}—and luxury real estate in Monaco was going for €60,000 a square foot. The parking space alone cost €250,000.

The floor was imported Italian marble, and the furnishings were midcentury modern. Abstract art hung on the walls, and floor-to-ceiling windows offered a panoramic view of the harbor.

It had an open architecture. The living room extended seamlessly into the dining room and futuristic kitchen. It was impeccably styled, with luxurious appointments. There was a large terrace that offered a breathtaking view of the Mediterranean.

The building had a concierge that could handle any request, night or day—shuttle service, valet parking, maid service, dry cleaning, car washing, babysitting—you name it. There was even a chef on demand, and a helipad atop the building.

This woman definitely didn't need to steal my kidneys and sell them on the black market. She didn't need to roll me for the contents of my wallet. I felt stupid for even harboring the thought, initially.

Katya's stiletto heels clacked against the tile as she sauntered to the minibar. "Can I offer you a drink?"

"Sure."

"What will it be?"

"Dealer's choice," I said, feeling adventurous.

She poured two shots of Jägermeister and handed one to me. She lifted her glass and toasted, "To new acquaintances."

"To new acquaintances," I said and slugged down the brown liquid that was like molten licorice.

I enjoyed the sweet, sharp taste.

Without warning, Katya leaned in close and planted her plump lips against mine. The taste of the Jäger lingered in her mouth, and our tongues became well acquainted.

After a blissful moment, she abruptly pushed me away and smiled. She spun around and sauntered toward the sliding glass door that led to the balcony. Her long fingers grabbed the bottom of her skirt and pulled the hem up over her hips. Her pert assets swayed from side to side, and my eyes widened at the glorious sight—she wasn't wearing any panties.

She moved to the edge of the balcony and leaned over, revealing everything she had to offer.

I wasn't stupid.

I knew a good invitation when I saw one, so I happily obliged her desires.

If anyone was looking, we gave them a hell of a show on the balcony. Katya's moans of ecstasy echoed in the night air, and I'm sure people down in the harbor could hear.

I think she liked the attention. And I was happy to indulge her.

When it was all said and done, she shimmied her skirt down over her hips, and I pulled up my pants. I leaned against the railing, enjoying the buzz of euphoria. The rush of chemicals filled my brain, better than any drug. My eyes took in the glimmering lights of the city, and I gazed at the horde of yachts docked in the harbor.

Katya excused herself for a moment and slipped back into the condo. She emerged a few moments later with a cigarette, two drinks, and a gold lighter bedazzled with diamonds.

She handed me another shot of Jäger. This time I decided to sip it.

She sparked the flint and the amber flame flickered, casting a warm glow on her face as she puffed the cigarette until the cherry glowed red. She drew in a lungful, then exhaled into the night air—a thick cloud of smoke billowing from her full lips.

She offered the cigarette to me.

"No thanks. I don't smoke."

"It's a terrible habit. I'm trying to quit. I've cut way down, but I refuse to give it up after sex. Especially good sex," she said with a satisfied glimmer in her eyes.

"I'm sure you say that to all your men."

She looked at me flatly. "I don't bullshit. I don't have to."

This woman didn't have to do anything she didn't want to.

"By now you've learned that I'm straightforward. I see what I want, and I take it."

"I've noticed."

"Life is too short for games. Why pretend? If you love some-one, tell them. If you want to sleep with someone, and the feeling is reciprocated, do it. Why deny yourself anything? Life is not a dress rehearsal. Don't save your best for later. This isn't a cell phone plan—the minutes don't roll over when you die."

It sounded reasonable, especially after several drinks and some great sex.

"This is a nice place," I said.

"Thank you. It's not very large, but it's my favorite of all my properties."

"How many do you have?"

"I have a few investment properties here in Monaco. One in London. One in Barcelona. One in Paris. And a condo in New York."

Suddenly, I felt poor.

"So, tell me what was it like?"

"What was *what* like?"

"Killing Bree Taylor."

My face twisted. "I didn't kill her."

In a seductive voice, she said, "It's just us. I won't tell."

She dropped to her knees and was quite persuasive in her attempts to extract a confession.

Words became difficult as she distracted me. Was this some type of weird role play? Should I play along with it? "Doesn't the thought of being alone with a potential killer frighten you?"

"It turns me on. Danger is stimulating, don't you think?"

Katya was seriously bat-shit crazy. But that made it all the more fun.

Stimulating indeed.

13

I was so absorbed in my thoughts that I didn't notice someone following me at first.

I had left Katya's apartment with mixed emotions. She made no bones about the fact she just wanted to sleep with me because I had been on TV and was the guy who had been having an affair with Bree Taylor. It would be a conversation piece for her at cocktail parties.

I sort of felt bad about taking advantage of my newfound celebrity, but not *that* bad. She did, after all, give great headspace.

It was shortly after midnight, and I walked down *Rue Grimaldi*, heading back to the *Hôtel Impérial*. The night air was cool, and I wished I had a light jacket when the breeze picked up. The leaves of the trees rustled in the wind. The street was desolate and covered with long shadows.

The last few days had been a whirlwind. I could see how this lifestyle would seriously mess with someone's head. I was nobody, and still people wanted something from me.

I was a novelty.

Something to gossip about.

I couldn't imagine being in the public eye 24/7. I hoped it would all die down soon. Though the attention wasn't *all* bad.

It didn't take long for me to realize the person behind me was drawing closer. I looked over my shoulder and saw a shadowy figure.

I stopped and turned around. I was in no mood to play games. That's when I saw the blade glimmer, reflecting the street light that hovered high above.

"You killed her!" the figure shouted.

I squinted my eyes, trying to see into the shadows. I wasn't particularly nervous. It was a girl with a knife. I could handle a knife. A gun, not so much.

She stepped forward, and the street light illuminated her face. I recognized her instantly. "Carolyn?"

Her face was red, and tears streamed down her cheek. Her fist clenched the handle of the knife. Rage boiled under her skin.

Okay, now I was a little nervous. Crazed, psychopathic stalker with a knife—a little more unpredictable.

"Carolyn, I didn't kill anyone."

"Bree didn't drown!" she said with conviction.

"Just put the knife down. And tell me why you think that. I don't think she drowned either."

The knife trembled in her hand.

"Carolyn, you don't want to hurt me. I was Bree's friend. I'm trying to find out what happened to her."

Her face crinkled with confusion, not sure what to do.

"I'm not the bad guy. Just put the knife down."

After a moment her grip slacked, and the knife clattered against the sidewalk. She broke down in jerking sobs.

I moved toward her and kicked the knife away. Then I put a delicate hand on her shoulder, trying to comfort her. "It's going to be okay."

"It's not okay. Bree is dead. And she's never coming back!"

"Are you here in Monaco with anyone?"

"No," she sobbed. "I'm by myself."

I didn't know how stable this woman was. Did she just have a fixation with the celebrity? Or was there some type of deeper neuroses?

I wanted to think she was harmless, but this was twice that I had seen her clutching a knife.

"I'm sorry," she mumbled. "I don't know what came over me. I'm just so mad." She wiped her eyes. "What happened?"

"I wish I knew."

"Bree couldn't have drowned," she said. "She was on the swim team in high school, and she almost made the Olympic team. There's no way."

"The authorities are saying she hit her head. She was probably unconscious when she was in the water." There I was, playing devil's advocate again.

"Someone hit her in the head," Carolyn said. The muscles in her jaw flexed.

I tended to agree with her. "Where were you the night she died? What did you do after you left the *Silver Screams?*"

"I went to *After Hours*. Had a few drinks. Met this guy, and we ended up back at his place."

"And *this guy* will verify this?"

Carolyn nodded.

"I'll need his name and address."

"I don't remember the specific address, but I think I can find his apartment again. His name was Sebastian."

14

"Have you lost your goddamn mind?" JD hissed.

"I think she might be able to help us," I said in a forceful whisper.

I had brought Carolyn back to the hotel. She waited in the hallway just outside the door.

"That chick is certifiable," JD said. "She pulled a knife on you twice, and your dead girlfriend had a restraining order against her. I'm not the sharpest tool in the shed, but even I know that's a red flag."

"She knows everything about Bree. And she doesn't think it was a drowning either." I told JD that Bree was damn near an Olympic swimmer.

That didn't seem to make much difference.

"I don't think she's really dangerous," I said, tentatively.

"Okay, great. If you say so. But if you wake up with your balls in a coffee cup on the nightstand, don't come crying to me."

"I'm not sleeping with her," I muttered.

I let out an exasperated sigh, then moved to the door and invited Carolyn into the room. JD flashed a nervous smile as I introduced her. I shot him a look that said *behave*.

"Carolyn is going to help us solve this case," I proclaimed.

"Are you two like, detectives?" she asked.

"We're Deputy Sheriffs in Coconut Key," JD replied.

"Oh," Carolyn said, meekly. "I just want you both to know, I will do anything to help bring Bree's killer to justice."

"We appreciate that," I said.

"She was really... special... to me."

"Did you two know each other?" I asked. "I mean, on a personal level?"

"Well, I'm obviously a huge fan. The first time I saw her in a movie I was blown away by her performance. She's magnetic. *Was* magnetic."

Her eyes filled with tears.

"I can't believe I have to talk about her in the past tense." She wiped her eyes and sniffled.

"When did you start..." I tried to think of a delicate way to put it, "focusing on her?"

She fidgeted, looking at the floor, embarrassed. "I know, I have a little problem with fixation. If you haven't noticed, I'm a little obsessive."

"No," JD said, his voice dripping with sarcasm. "I hadn't noticed that at all."

I shot him a look.

"I know, it's a problem. I'm in therapy, if that's what you're worried about. But, I just felt like from the moment I saw her, there was a connection between us. Our lives were destined to intertwine at some point. I'm not really psychic, but I get these feelings. You know, it's like I just know when something's going to happen."

"Can you tell me the lotto numbers?" JD asked.

Carolyn's eyes narrowed at him. "It's not like that."

"What's it like?" I asked.

"Like the night she died. I just knew something bad was going to happen. That's why I came to the boat to warn her."

JD glanced to me and made a subtle motion that he thought this woman was cuckoo.

"Supposing she was murdered, who had motive?" I asked.

"Savannah Skye," Carolyn said. "Without a doubt."

I met Savannah at the party, and I knew she didn't think too highly of Bree. She was on my short list of suspects as well.

"It was just announced in the trades today that she took over Bree's role in David Cameron's new film."

"I'd say that's motive," JD chimed.

"I'd like to know if she has an alibi," I said.

"Good luck talking to her?" JD said. "She'll be surrounded

by publicists and bodyguards, and I'm sure she won't say a thing without a lawyer."

"She has a film premiering at the festival tomorrow night," Carolyn added.

"It looks like we're going to Cannes," I said.

I sent Carolyn home, and JD locked the door behind her, flipped the deadbolt, and attached the chain. He wasn't taking any chances.

The next day we took a helicopter to Cannes. It was €160 each. The ride lasted a few minutes, and the helipad was a short 10-minute walk from the Palais.

I had never seen anything like it. There were movie stars everywhere, and gaggles of paparazzi followed them around, flashing their cameras. There were hordes of fans. Luxury yachts filled the harbor. It was a *Who's Who* of Hollywood. All of Los Angeles had been transplanted to the south of France for a few weeks.

I figured it must have made the traffic back in LA almost bearable.

JD and I weaved our way through the hordes of fans toward the red carpet, but we couldn't get close. The wall of photographers blocked access.

A limousine pulled to the curb and Savannah Skye stepped onto the red carpet to the roar of starstruck fans. She basked in the adoration, like a vampire bathing in blood. She sauntered down the red carpet, escorted by a man in a tuxedo. Questions were thrown at her about Bree's death, which overshadowed inquiries about her current film screening at the festival.

She maintained a fake smile and repeated the same answers over and over again. "It was such a tragedy. I'm heartbroken. We were such good friends. I will do my best to honor Bree's memory as I assume her role in David Cameron's film, *UltraMega*."

It was enough to make me sick listening to it.

She continued down the red carpet, stopping for interviews, posing for pictures. My plan was to get access to her later, at the after party.

JD and I left the Palais and walked down to the harbor. There were mega-yachts as far as the eye could see. They were full of revelers and tanned topless beauties catching the last rays of sunshine.

Someone came up to JD and asked for his autograph, mistaking him for an 80s rock star. He puffed up with excitement, more than happy to take on the role.

Within moments, a crowd had gathered around him, and JD signed autographs for the next 20 minutes.

"Vince," a man in a suit shouted. He plowed through the crowd and extended his hand. "Pete Mitchell, Inventive Artists Agency. We met a few years ago at Sandra Pollock's party."

Jack nodded, pretending to remember.

Pete was 35 with short curly blonde hair, and a fashionable amount of stubble on his chin. He wore a gray *Oberto* suit, a white button-down, and Prada sunglasses. "Are you here for the screening of Savannah's film?"

"Sort of," Jack said.

"Me too. But I can never sit through these things." He leaned in and spoke in a hushed tone. "Besides, I saw a rough cut a few months ago, and between you and me, it wasn't very good. I'm just gonna show up at the after party and tell Savannah how wonderful I thought her performance was."

"You and I are on the same wavelength," JD said.

"Listen, I'm having a little gathering aboard my yacht. I'd love it if you'd join us for a few minutes. We can pre-game, then head over to the after party."

"I believe that would work," JD said with a grin.

He introduced me to Pete, and a faint glimmer of recognition flickered in his eyes as he tried to place my face. He pretended that he knew who I was and smiled as we shook hands.

We followed him down the dock to his yacht. It was a 103 foot *SunTrekker*™ named *Eye for Talent*. The main deck aft opened into a luxurious salon with the staterooms below deck. It wasn't quite as nice as the *Silver Screams*, but it was no slouch.

Music pumped through speakers, and topless girls bounced around.

JD could barely contain himself.

Two girls were snorting lines off a glass coffee table.

It was *that* kind of party.

"Welcome aboard," Pete said. "Make yourself at home. Feel free to indulge your desires." Pete suddenly remembered something. "Oh, wait. You're clean now, right?"

JD nodded, assuming the role of a rehabbed, clean and sober rock star. "I swore off the hard drugs, but I won't turn down whiskey."

Pete looked to me, taking my order.

"Same."

He spun around and shouted to a waiter who hurried over with three glasses of fine whiskey.

Pete lifted his glass. "Too good times."

We clinked glasses and slugged the amber liquid down. It was smooth and sweet. Not too dry.

"If you'll excuse me, I need to mingle with my guests."

Pete smiled and drifted around the salon. He sat on the couch and did a bump with the girls.

"Who is that guy?" I whispered.

"Who the hell knows?"

"How long before he figures out you're not who he thinks you are?"

JD shrugged. "Let's drink up while we can."

15

B*e Someone* was an upscale bar not far from the Palais. JD and I walked with Pete and his bevy of coked up beauties a few blocks to the exclusive after party. Pete was on the guest list, which gave us access as part of his entourage.

Dance music pumped through speakers. There were fresh hors d'oeuvres and an open bar. The place was elegant and modern. JD and I made good use of the free drinks. You couldn't take a step without bumping into a celebrity.

It was starting to become normal.

We mixed and mingled, and Savannah finally arrived an hour later. She was swarmed by colleagues offering praise and congratulations. Despite Pete's dismissive comments, the film had received a warm reception at the festival, and the critics had been kind.

The club was dim and had a cozy vibe. Her publicist brought Savannah a drink, and she socialized for a while. I waited for a break in the action to approach.

"Outstanding performance," I said.

"Thank you. What was your favorite part?"

I hesitated a moment. "It's hard to choose, really. You are so mesmerizing on screen, I enjoyed all of it."

"You catch on quick," she said, well aware I was bullshitting. "You'll do fine in this town."

This town was a reference to Hollywood, and it didn't matter our geographical location.

She looked at me with her sultry eyes. "So, did you do it?"

She didn't seem the least bit intimidated or concerned.

"No. Of course not. Did you?"

She scoffed, acting like it was the most preposterous thing she'd ever heard. "Why would you even ask?"

"I gathered you two weren't the best of friends."

She gave me a fake smile. "Whatever gave you that impression? Bree was like a sister to me."

"I'm sure," I said, my voice dripping with sarcasm.

She took another sip of her drink and glanced around the club, looking for someone.

"What time did you leave the boat that night?" I asked.

She arched an eyebrow at me. "You can't be serious? Are you really asking this?"

"Satisfy my curiosity?"

"I know that Joel is trying to set up a deal for you around

town. But get this straight, if you use my name or likeness, or disparage me in any way, I will sue the pants off you."

"Are you trying to get me naked again?"

"You wish."

"So, your offer's not on the table anymore?"

"Which offer?" she asked, pretending to forget.

She knew damn good and well what she offered me that night on Bree's boat.

Savannah's eyes found her publicist across the room and she flashed her a look that said *save me*.

"So, I take it you don't want me to write a part for you."

Her eyes snapped back to me. That piqued her interest. "What part?"

"I'm still tossing around ideas. I don't quite have the ending yet."

Her publicist stormed to us, knowing that something was wrong. She had sandy blonde hair and wore a pantsuit and thin wire-frame glasses.

She was all business.

She grabbed Savannah's arm, gently, and started to pull her away. "Please excuse us, she has many guests to speak with."

"We were just talking about the night Bree was murdered," I said.

That stopped her in her tracks.

The publicist forced a smile. "Yes, such a tragedy. Savannah is very broken up about it."

"I can see that."

The publicist's eyes narrowed at me. "She wishes she could have been there to save Bree and regrets leaving the party. She had another engagement to attend to. You can imagine how difficult that must be, knowing your best friend died shortly after you left her in the company of a strange individual."

"I can imagine," I said. "What engagement did Savannah attend afterward?"

The publicist answered sternly. "Savannah was at a party aboard De Campo's yacht. There are plenty of witnesses that can corroborate her appearance there. If you have any further questions, please feel free to contact my office, or Savannah's attorney."

The publicist ushered Savannah away and spoke to a security guard. Within seconds a big bouncer hovered over me. He was damn near 7 feet tall and twice as wide as I was. He had a low booming voice that rumbled my chest when he spoke, even over the music. "You're not on the guest list."

He motioned toward the door.

I glanced around, looking for Pete, but I couldn't find him in the increasingly dense party. I looked at JD and said, "I'm with him."

"He can stay," the bouncer said, mistaking Jack for a rock star. "You gotta go."

The bouncer grabbed my arm and started pulling me

toward the door. He dragged me through the crowd, and I thought it was best if I didn't start trouble with him. He was just about to toss me onto the street when Joel intervened. "It's okay. He's a client of mine."

The bouncer frowned at Joel.

"Run along," Joel said shooing the large man away with his hand. "If I say he can stay, he can stay."

"Yes, Mr. Järvi," the bouncer said as he skulked away.

"Look at you," Joel said with delight. "Fitting in well, I see. You're not a celebrity until you get kicked out of swanky parties."

"When in Rome."

"You're blowing up. Front page of every gossip rag on the planet."

"Great," I said, disappointedly.

"I want to strike while the iron is hot. There is a lot of interest in this right now, and I think I can spin that to our advantage."

"Hang on. I never agreed to any of this."

"Trust me, you want me as your agent. People in this town kill to have me as their agent." He thought about it for a moment. "Sorry, that was a bad analogy."

"I'm not interested."

"Yes you are. Everyone's interested. Besides, I'm a good friend to have. I can open a lot of doors."

"What do you have in mind?"

"All the talk shows are begging for an appearance. Next week, this story won't even be news. But this week, I think we can line up a seven-figure deal at a major studio. The script practically writes itself. When are you planning on heading back to the States?"

I shrugged. "I don't think Bree drowned. I'm not leaving until I get to the bottom of this," I replied.

"Ooh, I love it. *Murder suspect searches for movie star's killer.*"

I rolled my eyes.

"Between you and me, I don't think she drowned either," Joel said. "Listen, I've got the best writer in town working on the treatment. He'll have something to pitch to the studios soon. I'll be back in Monaco tomorrow. Let's get together, go over the concept, then pitch it."

"We don't know how the story ends yet," I said with a healthy dose of sarcasm.

"Doesn't matter. We're just selling the concept."

"Let me ask you something. Did you care about Bree at all?"

Joel gasped. "I cared about her very much. She was a dear friend. We have an opportunity to tell her story, and I think it needs to be told. Besides, why leave money on the table?"

I paused, not sure I liked the idea of this.

"You've got something I need," I said.

He flashed a cocky grin. "I'm sure I do, but I don't sleep with my clients."

My eyes narrowed at him. "Access."

"That's what I've been telling you."

"I think somebody at her party killed her that night," I said. "You help me find out who did it, and I'll sign your contract."

Joel smiled. "I think we have a deal."

"Let's get one thing out of the way first," I said. "Where were you at the time of her death?"

"Ooh, the plot thickens," Joel said excitedly.

16

"I can tell you exactly where I was," Joel said. "I left the party and hooked up with an actor."

"I thought you didn't date clients?"

"Not my client," Joel said with a mischievous grin.

"Want to tell me who it was?"

"I can't reveal that information," Joel said.

"So, you want me to take your word for it?"

"Any good relationship is based on trust. You want to be my client? We need a mutual trust."

"You're the one who wanted me as a client, remember?"

Joel thought about this for a moment. "Okay. If you say a word, I'll deny till death." Joel whispered a name in my ear.

I raised my eyebrows in surprise. "Really?"

"Really!"

"I need to verify that."

"Good luck. He's certainly not going to admit to anything."

"That puts you in a bit of a predicament, doesn't it?" I said.

"What possible motive would I have for killing my best client? I stand to make considerably less money now that she's not around."

He eyed me suspiciously. "Where were you?"

"Asleep in the master suite."

"See. You don't have an alibi either. Do you want my help, or don't you?"

I sighed and reluctantly resigned myself to the fact that I would have to trust an agent. It sounded like an oxymoron.

I was no farther along than when I started.

"What about Zazzle?" I asked. "He seemed to blame Bree for the breakup of his band."

"Why don't you ask him yourself. He's right over there," Joel said, pointing across the dim room to a booth in the corner.

Zazzle was surrounded by groupies. There was a bottle of whiskey on the table, and they were snorting a fine white powder that I was pretty sure was cocaine.

I strolled over to the table and was greeted with an angry glare. "What the fuck do you want?"

"I was wondering if you knew anything about Bree's death?"

"Just what I see on the news." Zazzle said. "Now get the fuck out of here before I kick your teeth in."

"I recall you trying that before. It didn't work out so well for you."

The muscles in Zazzle's jaw flexed.

"Where were you after the party that night?"

The rockstar's face crinkled up, and he shared a glance with his groupies. "Who is this guy?" His glassy eyes looked back to me. "Weren't you were arrested? Aren't you a *person of interest*?"

"It seems like you had a pretty big beef with her," I said.

"She was a raging fucking bitch. She broke up the greatest rock band since Led Zeppelin."

I scoffed. "That's a bold statement."

"It's the truth. Sue me. That bitch seriously pulled a Yoko Ono."

"Something tells me you are far from the Beatles."

Zazzle snarled at me. He made a move like he was going to get up, but thought better of it. "Why do you care?"

"I don't know," I said. "I just do."

"You didn't mean anything to her. You were just another in a long list. Hate to pop your cherry, pal."

"You know, the sad thing is, I used to like your music until I met you."

He muttered something at me as I walked away.

This was getting nowhere.

Zazzle had dozens of groupies that would be willing to say

they had spent the night with him. I was trying to conduct a murder investigation with no authority behind me. I had no teeth. No power. And all the celebrities thought they were untouchable.

And they probably were.

Nobody wanted to push the issue. Nobody was interested in the truth. Bree's death had been wrapped up with a nice bow. A simple explanation. An accident. There was no murder. Nothing to worry about. And everybody wanted it to stay that way.

I began to wonder what the hell I was doing?

Once the open bar ended, the parties thinned out. Joel invited us to another party on a movie star's yacht in the harbor.

The same people seemed to move from venue to venue, with a minor change in the supporting characters.

It all started to blur together. Drink after drink, yacht after yacht, pretty girl after pretty girl.

It was easy to become numb to it all. It was performance art, and each venue was a stage. Nothing was real, and everyone put on a façade. The endless mix of booze and drugs made it a surreal dreamlike fantasy world. There was no future, and there was no past. Nothing really mattered. There were no consequences.

Not when you were ultra-famous or super-rich.

One moment blended into the next. Days could go by. Then weeks. Then months. Then years. It was an insulated bubble of exclusive parties and excessive indulgences. You were either somebody, or hanging onto somebody. The has-beens and the never-was-beens weren't allowed.

Yet everyone thought they would be a star forever.

I ran into Liam on De Campo's boat. His eyes filled with disdain when he saw me. He looked at his watch as I approached and said, "Isn't your 15 minutes up by now?"

"I've got a few minutes left."

"Enjoy it while it lasts."

He started to walk away, but I grabbed his arm.

He flashed me a look that said *I'll press charges if you don't release me*.

"I'm just trying to find out what happened that night."

"She drowned. Let it go."

"You don't really believe that, do you?"

"I don't know what happened. But if somebody *did* kill her, I'm probably looking at the prime suspect." His eyes burned into mine.

"Do you think I'd be walking the streets now if the police had anything concrete?"

He glared at me.

"I can't seem to get a straight answer out of anybody, but I'll ask the question anyway. Where were you when she died?"

"I was with my wife. She's right over there if you want to talk to her." He pointed her out in the crowd.

I talked to her later, and she confirmed Liam's story. But I didn't expect otherwise. If you wanted to stay happily married to your husband, you'd sure as hell confirm his alibi.

"You knew Bree well," I said. "Is there anybody who would have wanted to do her harm? Besides Savannah or Zazzle?"

"This is Hollywood," Liam said. "Everyone has enemies."

"There was a guy at the party that night. Linen suit. Tan. Blonde highlights. Bree seemed to have an intense conversation with him. She didn't look happy about it. Neither did he."

Liam thought about it. "Vincent Villeneuve?"

"Yeah, that's him."

"Art dealer. Mostly contemporary, but sometimes he can get some rare classics."

"Picassos?"

Liam's face twisted. "She paid way too much for that."

"That could be what they were fighting about," I suggested. "Did she have a case of buyer's remorse?"

"I told her not to buy it. She couldn't afford it." He looked around and made sure no one was eavesdropping. "If this ends up in the trades, I'll kill you." Then he said in a hushed tone, "She was on the verge of bankruptcy."

That hung in the air.

But it didn't come as a total surprise. Though it was still hard to wrap my head around how someone who made $20 million a picture could go bankrupt.

I thought back to the first time I saw the Picasso hanging on the bulkhead in the master suite. Then it dawned on me. I hadn't noticed it when I collected my bags after I'd been released from jail.

I didn't say anything just yet. Somebody had stolen the painting. Liam had access. My mind raced with possibilities.

"Who is handling Bree's estate?" I asked.

Liam hesitated a moment. "That's where things get complicated. She died without a will. She was 27 years old. How many 27-year-olds do you know that are on top of their estate planning? I had been urging her to take care of it."

"So she died intestate?

"And her death in Monaco complicates matters. I'm still trying to determine how the assets here will have to be settled, and which law will apply. Monaco recently changed their code in 2017, so the law of Bree's nationality may apply. Her attorney is handling that. I've contacted her mother and her sister. But her mother is an invalid and unable to travel. Her sister should be arriving tomorrow."

"When did she purchase the Picasso?"

"Last week. Why?"

"It's missing," I said.

Liam's face went pale.

"What do you mean it's missing?"

"When I got my bag, it wasn't in the master suite."

"Are you sure?" His eyes were full of skepticism.

"I have an eye for noticing detail. I was just so frazzled at the time, it didn't register."

Liam's face tensed.

"Who had access to the boat?"

He thought for a moment. "Me, obviously. Bree's Attorney. Her agent. But no one was there unattended but me."

I gave him a look.

"No. I didn't take it, if that's what you're thinking?"

I shrugged. "Somebody took it. If you don't believe me, maybe you should go see for yourself."

17

JD and I took a helicopter with Liam back to Monaco. Liam was determined to see with his own eyes that the Picasso was missing.

The rotor blades whirled overhead, and the city lights glimmered below. Every time I was aboard a helicopter it brought me back to my days as a Special Operator. I'm not going to say I miss those days—who really misses being cold, tired, hungry, and far away from home? But it made me a little nostalgic.

We landed on the helipad and took a cab down to the harbor. Liam flew into a rage as we stepped into the master suite of Bree's yacht.

The Picasso was gone.

"God dammit!" Liam practically frothed at the mouth. His face was beet red, and the veins in his temples pulsed. He clenched his fists and paced about compartment.

He seemed genuinely upset.

Either he didn't steal the painting, or he was a damn good actor. I wasn't sure which.

Liam put his hand to his face and rubbed his chin, deep in thought.

"Who knew the painting was there?" I asked.

"Me, Bree, you, Vincent, and Joel."

"I didn't take it," I said.

There was another long pause.

"Thanks for bringing this to my attention." He paused. "Listen, I'm sorry I've been so abrasive with you. Bree was an important part of my life. I'm having trouble processing her death. I really want to get to the bottom of this."

I appreciated his apology.

"If you'll excuse me, I need to make some phone calls." Liam motioned toward the hatch.

JD and I left the master suite and walked up to the main deck.

Liam followed.

"Perhaps we should pay Vincent Villeneuve's gallery a visit?" I suggested.

"I'll handle this," Liam said, sternly.

I raised my hands in surrender. "Whatever you say."

I thanked him for indulging my curiosity. JD and I left and strolled down the dock.

A message from Isabella dinged on my phone. It was a file containing Bree's text messages.

I gazed at the file on the display and hesitated a moment before opening it. I felt bad about invading her privacy. But, maybe it would provide insight.

Isabella had dug up texts from the last 30 days. One of her *nerd herd* had hacked into the cell carrier system and retrieved the data.

It wasn't legal, and anything I found wouldn't be admissible in any court of law. But this wasn't about the law.

This was about justice.

I opened the file and sifted through the messages. It was mostly chitchat between friends. Gossip. Chats with her agent—discussions about upcoming roles and career opportunities. There were several texts from Liam, advising her to take a more conservative approach with her finances.

Then I found the good stuff.

There was a heated exchange with Vincent. Bree wanted her money back for the Picasso.

The painting was a forgery.

My jaw dropped.

Apparently she had the painting authenticated by a renowned expert who raised serious concerns. Bree threatened to go public if Vincent didn't refund her money immediately.

That would ruin his reputation.

And it probably wasn't the only forgery he had passed off as real.

Vincent did business with everybody. Movie stars, tech billionaires, Russian oligarchs, and mobsters looking for safe investments.

A motive began to form.

If Vincent had sold a fake to a ruthless gangster, and that information became public, he was as good as dead.

That's definitely a motive for murder in my book.

Vincent would have done anything to keep her quiet. He probably stole the painting back for fear that it would be appraised during the probate of Bree's estate. The forgery would have surely been discovered during that process.

It was a plausible theory. But that's all it was.

I needed proof.

JD and I walked back toward the hotel. I figured we'd swing by Vincent's gallery in the morning and see what we could sniff out.

We headed up *Avenue du Port*. The moonlight bathed the street in a pale glow. It was a nice evening.

A nice evening to die.

A car slowed as it pulled to the curb beside us. The window rolled down, and a hand stuck out. The hand was holding a pistol with a suppressor attached to the barrel.

Muzzle flash flickered, and a bullet snapped across the side-walk. I could feel the copper projectile displace the air as it zipped inches from my body and smacked into the brick building beside me.

Chips of brick and mortar showered.

I grabbed JD, pulling him to the ground, taking cover behind a parked car.

Several more bullets flew through the air. The muffled *pop, pop, pop,* echoing down the street. Glass shattered and metal pinged as stray bullets peppered parked cars.

JD and I scampered into an alley as bullets streaked all around us, sending chips of brick and concrete hurtling through the air. We disappeared into the shadows of the alley and kept running.

The assassin's tires squealed as the car escaped into the night.

We exited the alley, crossed the next street, then darted to another alley and kept going.

Our footsteps echoed off the alley walls as we sprinted away. My heart pounded. My quads burned.

Jack's chest heaved for breath, and sweat misted on his face. He wasn't in quite the shape he had been back in the day.

We finally stopped and caught our breath.

"You okay?" I asked.

His face looked pale, and I could tell something was wrong. My eyes caught sight of a spot of crimson, blossoming on his shirt.

He'd been hit!

18

J ack lifted his shirt. He had a layer of padding where there used to be ripped abs. His winter coat of barbecue and beer may just have saved his life.

"God damn, that stings!"

Blood seeped out of the wound, but it didn't gush. The entry wound was just lateral of the midline between the rectus abdominis and the obliques.

I wasn't a doctor, but I'd seen enough combat injuries. I knew my way around gunshot wounds fairly well. This one wasn't as bad as it could have been.

I poked around the wound with my fingertip.

"Quit that!" he yelped.

I could feel the slug embedded in his skin. But, in my amateur opinion, it hadn't punctured the peritoneal space.

That would've been a disaster.

Gut wounds are some of the worst. When a bullet punctures

the abdominal wall and rips through the intestines, spilling bile, it creates an environment ripe for infection. Even with the proper medical treatment, gut wounds can often cause sepsis.

With today's resistant strains of bacteria, even the most powerful antibiotics are becoming less and less effective.

This wasn't a direct shot.

The bullet must have ricocheted off the wall, then punctured the skin.

I helped JD sit down, leaning against the alley wall. "We need to get you to a hospital."

"Nonsense. I don't do hospitals. We just need to dig the little son-of-a-bitch out and stitch me up."

I rolled my eyes.

JD was a tough bastard, but he needed medical attention.

I called a cab, and we zipped across town to an emergency room. Jack kept pressure on the wound, but the oozing blood still stained the cab's leather seats.

We staggered into the ER, and the cab driver helped. He took off before I had a chance to pay him. The nurses triaged JD, taking blood pressure, and monitoring vitals. He was put on a gurney and wheeled into a treatment room.

We didn't have to wait, due to the nature of his injury. The ER wasn't that busy, anyway.

The craggy peaks of JD's heartbeat pulsed on the bedside monitor. Nurses swarmed around him, wearing sterile clothes and purple nitrile gloves. They started him on IV fluids. The clear bag of saline hung from a stand by the side of the bed. JD winced when the nurse stuck the IV portal into the vein on the back of his hand. She covered the site with a clear adhesive patch.

With a pair of blunt-end scissors, a nurse cut off JD's shirt.

His face crinkled with distress. "What are you doing?"

"The shirt and the pants have to come off."

"At least by me dinner first," JD said. "I'm not that easy."

She wasn't amused.

"That's my favorite shirt, by the way."

"Think of it as an excuse to update to a more contemporary style," the nurse said, dryly.

JD's scowled at her subtle assault upon his fashion sense.

A doctor entered into the room and his eyes glanced to the vital signs monitor. A nurse updated him on the situation.

The doctor was maybe 35 years old. He had curly brown hair, green eyes, wore teal scrubs, and a white lab coat. His nose was long and angular, like a shark fin, and he had a narrow jawline. He spoke English with a thick accent. "Do you know what type of weapon you were shot with?"

"I didn't get a chance to inspect it," JD said with a hint of sarcasm.

"9mm, I think," I said.

"At what distance were you shot?" the doctor inquired.

"Close enough," JD said.

"Maybe 20 feet," I clarified. "I think the bullet ricocheted."

"Do you know who shot you?"

"My ex-wife is not in the country, so I think I can rule her out."

The doctor was not amused.

"Vitals are stable," a nurse said in French.

"What were you doing at the time of the shooting?"

A perplexed look twisted on JD's face. "What the hell does that matter? I was minding my own damn business."

The doctor and nurses inspected JD's body for additional wounds. Bullet holes can be remarkably small at times and can appear not much larger than a mole.

JD groaned as they rolled him onto his side to check his back and hindquarters.

"Hey now," JD said as a nurse poked and prodded around his bum.

I could've done without seeing JD's ass.

The nurses returned JD to a supine position, and the doctor examined the entry wound.

JD grimaced as the gloved finger pushed around the bloody wound.

"Probably superficial, but let's get an abdominal CT just in case," the doctor ordered.

An X-ray tech rolled JD out of the room and down the hall

to imaging. A few minutes later he was back in the room. The CT had confirmed the doctors initial suspicion.

The doctor numbed Jack with a local anesthetic and cleaned the area and debrided necrotic flesh. The nurses used a retractor to hold the wound open, and the doctor removed the twisted bullet from the fatty part of the abdomen with a pair of forceps.

He held the bullet up to view so JD could see. The bloody thing was twisted and mangled.

Jack had gotten lucky. There was no major damage. No rupture of the abdominal wall.

The doctor asked JD if he wanted to keep the bullet as a souvenir.

"Hell yes!" JD said.

The doctor stitched him up and prescribed a course of antibiotics for the next 3 days, as well as some pain medication.

The incident had been reported to local authorities, and by the time JD was nearing discharge, Inspector Géroux showed up and started asking questions. "Can you tell me what happened?"

"It's not illegal to get shot, is it?" JD asked.

"No. But shooting someone is. What can you tell me about the incident?"

"A car drove by and opened fire," I said.

"Make? Model? License plate?"

"4 door, late-model, black sedan," I said. "I didn't get much more than that."

"Any idea why you two might have been targeted?" Géroux asked.

There could've been several reasons why we were targeted. Maybe somebody didn't like us snooping around? Maybe the cartel had seen me on television and had sent a hit squad? I would likely never know, and I didn't feel like discussing it with Géroux.

"My personality is so radiant, some people just want to snuff it out," JD said.

The inspector was not amused.

"This is a very safe city," Géroux said. "We pride ourselves on that fact. Yet trouble seems to follow you, Mr. Wild."

"What can I say? Mystery and intrigue surrounds me."

"Then perhaps it should surround you somewhere else?" the inspector said, urging me to leave town. "Monaco has an image to protect. This kind of thing is not good for business, and it makes the residents feel uncomfortable."

"Believe me, I feel pretty uncomfortable right now," JD said. "I'm not going to tell you how to do your job, but it seems like you've got a few murderers running around out there. Maybe that's where you should focus your attention?"

Géroux's eyes narrowed at him. He was silent for a long moment. "If you two can think of any additional details about the attack, please contact me."

I assured him we would.

Géroux left, and JD didn't want to stay in the hospital any longer than necessary. The hospital typically discharged superficial wound patients the same day. Gunshot wounds involving bones, or deeper structures, required a multi-day stay.

I paid the bill, and we caught a cab back to the hotel. Transferring in and out of the car was painful for Jack, and he winced with pain. It hurt every time he flexed, and each turn and bump in the road tugged at his stitches.

By the time we got back to our room, JD's abdomen was black and blue. The bruising had finally set in. I had filled his prescription at a 24 hour pharmacy near the hospital while he waited for his discharge papers. JD popped two more pills of hydrocodone with acetaminophen. He washed them down with a glass of whiskey and crawled into bed.

Jack groaned like he was dying.

"Don't be such a wuss. You've been shot before."

"But at least I got to shoot back then. This time I had to run away like a little bitch."

"Don't you mean *waddle* away?"

His eyes narrowed at me. "Shut it. It's a good thing I had a little extra padding. Besides, haven't you heard? Dad-bod is in. Chicks love it."

"I'm just saying, someone your age should be mindful of excess abdominal fat."

"Respect your elders, young man," he chided. "Besides. My cholesterol is perfect. It's a proven fact beef brisket is good for the heart. Keto, bitch!"

I rolled my eyes. "Please, you eat carbs."

"Beer doesn't count," he insisted.

"We just ate pizza?" I said incredulous.

"Splurge day," he said, dismissively.

"Every day is a splurge day for you."

"YOLO."

"Are you allowed to say that when you're over 50?"

His eyes narrowed at me. "All the more reason to live for the moment."

He smiled.

I chuckled and shook my head at his bullshit. JD didn't much look after his health and didn't seem to give it a second thought. Jack planned on eating and drinking whatever he wanted until the widow-maker took him out. In truth, he was more likely to die from a gunshot from a jealous husband than a cheeseburger. And I think that's the way he hoped he would go.

Jack woke up sore as hell in the morning and instantly reached for another round of the hydrocodone.

"Go easy on that stuff," I cautioned. "Those opioids will block you up."

JD scowled at me. "I'll go easy when this stops hurting. Who are you, my mother?"

"Well, you are a child."

He sneered at me.

I left the room, went downstairs, and grabbed breakfast. The food was good, but the coffee was shit. It had been sitting too long and was over-heated.

I brought a plate back to the room for JD. "Will you be okay while I go pay our little art dealer friend a visit?"

"I'll go with you," JD said.

My face twisted. "The hell you will. Stay here and take it easy."

"I'm fine. It's a scratch." He tried to sit up and winced with pain. "Okay, maybe I'll sit this one out."

I chuckled.

JD picked up the phone and dialed guest services. "Can you send up an extra pillow and some more towels? Thank you."

"Try not to get into any trouble while I'm gone."

JD grinned, mischievously.

Vincent's art gallery was only two blocks from the hotel. It was a beautiful morning, and I stopped at a coffee shop across the street from the hotel to get a caffeine fix before heading east to the gallery. I had to put the horrid, stale hotel coffee behind me.

I grabbed a tall cup of coffee, then strolled down the block toward the gallery. It was another beautiful morning.

I knew something was wrong as I rounded the corner.

A crowd gathered around, and police cars with flashing blue lights were parked near the entrance to the gallery.

19

I asked an onlooker, "What happened?"

She shrugged. "I'm not sure. I think there was some kind of break in, or something. A man was killed."

I pushed through the crowd and peered into the large glass windows of the gallery.

Vincent lay dead on the floor enveloped by a pool of blood.

A forensics photographer took pictures, illuminating the gallery with flashes of brilliant light. Uniformed police officers kept onlookers at bay, while an investigative team bagged and tagged evidence.

Inspector Géroux hovered near the body, talking with a colleague. His eyes randomly caught sight of me peering into the window.

His face crinkled with frustration. He excused himself from his current conversation and marched out of the gallery. He found me in the crowd. "What are you doing here?"

I smiled. "Just enjoying my coffee and a short stroll."

"Do you know anything about this?"

"Only what you're willing to tell me."

His stern eyes gazed at me for a moment, then he said, "Come with me."

I followed him into the gallery, and he pointed at the body. "Do you know this man?"

I shrugged. "Not really."

He gave me a dirty look.

"I've never met him, but he was at Bree's party the night of her death. I've recently learned that she purchased a piece of art from him which turned out to be a forgery."

His brow lifted with surprise. "And how do you know this?"

"I hear things. I know people. They know people."

Géroux eyed me suspiciously for a moment. "Who are you?"

"I'm just a guy who was supposed to be on vacation. Then things took a turn."

"I ran a background check on you when you were detained. The profile doesn't fit. It's too clean. Too perfect."

I said nothing.

"I have a friend in the DGSE," he said.

He let it hang there for a moment.

The *Direction Générale de la Sécurité Extérieure* (General

Directorate for External Security) was the French equivalent
of the British MI6 and the American CIA.

"He thinks you could be CIA. Or, perhaps, a private
contractor?"

I said nothing.

"I believe we could help each other. But we must be very
honest with one another."

"Have you come across a Picasso on the premises?"

A glimmer of recognition sparkled in his eyes. "Oddly
enough, there was one in the storage area. Come this way."

He led me into the back of the gallery where hundreds of
paintings were stored. He showed me the painting that had
been hanging in Bree's master suite. I filled him in on its
history.

"Are you telling me that it is a fake?"

"That's exactly what I'm telling you. I suspect, if you analyze
other masterworks here, you may find more forgeries."

"That would certainly make Mr. Villeneuve a target,"
Inspector Géroux said. "This was meant to look like a
burglary gone wrong."

I told him that Bree was threatening to expose Vincent, and
that could have provided a motive for her murder.

He agreed.

Without saying as much, I gathered Géroux had been pres-
sured to wrap up Bree's case in a hasty fashion. But I sensed
he had his own suspicions.

"You think Vincent killed Bree, don't you?" Géroux asked.

"It seems highly probable."

"That gives you motive to kill Vincent, doesn't it?" he asked casually.

I scoffed. *Not this again?* "If you want to know my where-abouts this morning, I was at the hotel with my friend. You know where I was last night," I said. "You and I both know I'm not a very good suspect for this."

Géroux gave a subtle, apologetic nod. "I must do my due diligence."

"I understand."

"How long do you plan on staying in Monaco?"

"I told myself I would stay until the circumstances surrounding Bree's death became clear."

"And are they clear to you?"

"I don't know. Vincent certainly had motive."

"But you're not convinced?"

"Perhaps we will never know? "

He paused. "Who do you think was trying to kill you last night?"

"I have my ideas, but they are just guesses."

"You're an interesting man, Mr. Wild. You seem to be adept at making both friends and enemies."

"People either love me or hate me," I said with a grin.

We shook hands, and Inspector Géroux escorted me out of the gallery.

"I may contact you with further questions."

I smiled sincerely. "Happy to help."

I strolled back to the hotel and sipped on my coffee that was lukewarm by now.

JD was up and about by the time I returned to the hotel room. Despite his injury, he was surprisingly chipper. He held up a pain pill. "I discovered that three of these little bastards, plus a glass of whiskey will just about make my pain nonexistent."

"You're not supposed to drink with those."

His face twisted with a dismissive scowl. "Please. Those warnings are just for amateurs. I'm a seasoned professional."

"That acetaminophen is really bad for your liver."

"I'm just seeing if my liver will respond to the challenge," JD said. "It's like going to the gym and working out. The heavier you lift, the bigger your muscles get."

JD knew better.

My phone rang, and I pulled the device from my pocket. It was my *agent* calling. "Meet me at the casino in 20 minutes."

"Why?"

"I have a meeting with the head of a major studio. She wants to meet you. She likes the concept."

I let Joel know that Vincent was dead, and that I thought he probably killed Bree.

"Did you kill him?" Joel asked in an almost gleeful tone.

"No."

"Well, we can take dramatic license in the movie," he replied with a hint of disappointment.

I told him I'd meet him there and hung up the phone.

JD insisted on tagging along, despite my protests.

"I feel fine. What could go wrong? I'm just gonna play a little blackjack. Maybe a few slots. What am I gonna do, tear open my stitches pulling a slot machine lever?"

"Maybe you've forgotten, there's someone out there trying to kill us."

"They're trying to kill you. Everybody loves me," he muttered, full of himself.

I rolled my eyes.

We caught a cab over to the casino. It was too far to walk in JD's current condition.

The casino looked like a palace, fit for a king. The exquisite architecture was lavish—elegant Beaux-Arts design with 19th-century flair. The main entryway was lined with marble columns and had a high vaulted ceiling with a stained glass skylight. There were intricately decorated panels on the walls. A *Formula X* car was on display in the center of the entry hall.

In the gambling areas, the floors were covered with an intricately woven silk rug. You couldn't walk into this building and not feel like you stepped onto the set of a James Bond movie.

Roulette wheels spun, slot machines chimed, and dealers shuffled cards. It didn't have the cheap, overstimulated feel of a Vegas casino. There were no tacky lights, no flashing neon. Instead, magnificent chandeliers hung from the ceiling. Gold accents and crown moulding lined the opulent palace.

The entry fee was €10—a paltry sum compared to the dollar amount the high-rollers dropped. The whole city was the playground of the rich and famous, and nothing symbolized that more than the casino.

The wheels turn behind JD's eyes. I knew exactly what he was thinking. I had to admit, I couldn't wait to get a seat at a poker table and try my hand.

20

W
e met with the studio exec at the bar. Susan was considerably younger than I expected. Early 30s, brunette, brown eyes. We had a few drinks and talked for half an hour about everything but movies. The pitch about the story never came up, though JD did mention that he got shot the night before and eagerly showed off his stitches.

"Just so you know," Joel said, finally getting around to business. "Susan has the power to green-light any picture up to $125 million. Over that, it needs committee approval."

"Everything needs committee approval," Susan said. "We do most things by focus groups. But, when I see something I like, my input counts very heavily."

She made no bones about the power she wielded. Like many top-level executives, she had launched dozens of careers, and ended scores of others. The biggest stars on the planet would grovel at her feet.

I was nice to her, but I certainly didn't kiss her ass.

"How did you get into the business?" I asked.

"I grew up in Florida, went to NYU film school, then got a job in the mailroom of IAA. That's where I met Joel." Then she said aside, "Honestly, I was a failed actor, and I decided quickly that the life of an agent wasn't for me. I got an internship with a major studio. My boss liked me, hired me full-time. I followed him to a new studio, and when he got fired, I took over."

"Something tells me you don't have a lot of job security," I said.

She chuckled. "We're all one flop away from the unemployment line. Saying *no* to a project means that you keep your job. Saying *yes* means your neck is on the line."

"I don't suppose you say *yes* very often."

A flirtatious glint sparkled in her eyes. "In regard to film projects, no. But I'm not immune to persuasive argument."

There was a pause as she sipped her wine.

"So, Joel thinks you have a potential story."

"Honestly, this meeting was Joel's idea. I couldn't care less if we do business or not. I'm just trying to find out who killed Bree."

Joel cringed.

"Were you two close?" she asked.

"We had an interesting 24 hours."

"I really liked her," Susan said. "She was one of the few actresses that I could have a real conversation with. She never seemed to have any agenda. She knew she was a star and didn't have to prove it to anybody."

I raised a toast. "To Bree."

We all clinked glasses.

"To Bree," they answered.

"So, are you staying for the Grand Prix?" Susan asked. It seemed to be the default question everyone asked when they couldn't think of anything else to say.

"I don't know."

"Do you follow racing at all?"

"Yeah."

"I'm a big *Formula X*™ fan," Susan said.

"I enjoy it," I said.

"I've got a season pass and I watch it on my iPad. But it has gotten a little predictable. Is there any doubt that Mercedes, Ferrari, or Red Bull will be on the podium this year?"

I laughed. "They need to do what *MotoXP*™ did—offer concessions to teams without podiums. The race results in *MotoXP* are much more unpredictable. Keeps a level playing field."

She agreed.

We chatted for a few minutes, then the meeting came to an end. Susan thanked us for our time, and Joel gave me a subtle nod that we would talk later. He stayed at the bar with her while JD and I headed toward the poker tables.

We got some game chips from the cashier and sat down at a game of Texas Hold 'em Ultimate. All the games here were played against the dealer. Things started off well, but quickly went south. And within half an hour, I had burned through all of our chips.

JD was astonished, and so was I. "What the hell is wrong with you?"

I shrugged. "Off day."

"You never lose."

"Yeah, well, shit happens."

We headed back to the bar with dejected looks on our faces. Another round of whiskey would take the edge off. Along the way, my eye caught a glimmering object on the floor. I knelt down and picked up a gold lighter that was studded with diamonds.

I recognized it instantly.

It had the initials K.T. on it.

I grinned and slipped it into my back pocket. Maybe I'd bump into Katya and return it. If not, I figured I'd turn it in at the bar, but I got sidetracked when I bumped into Joel.

"Susan loved you both. But she doesn't want to do a biopic of Bree. Nor does she want to turn it into a true crime documentary series."

"Oh, well," I said, feeling relieved. "You win some, you lose some. It's probably for the best."

Joel had a mischievous grin. "I didn't say she wasn't interested in working with you. She wants to develop a series.

Former spy and his trusty sidekick solve crimes around coastal locations. There will be mystery, action, sex, intrigue, and comedy. She wants you both to be her guest to the Grand Prix."

JD grinned. "Looks like we're staying in Monaco for another few days."

"If we live that long," I said.

A text from Carolyn buzzed my phone. *[Meet me at TBD. We need to talk]*.

[About what?]

[Not over text].

21

We met Carolyn at a coffee shop not far from our hotel. She wasn't alone. The woman she was with wore a wide-brimmed hat, oversized sunglasses, and her hair was styled in a sleek blonde bob that hung just above her shoulders. At a close glance, I realized it was a wig.

This woman didn't want to be recognized.

They were seated in a booth toward the back of the shop. The blonde looked around, nervously. Then it hit me—this was Liam's wife, Elena.

Light jazz filtered through overhead speakers, and the smell of fresh coffee was divine. The subtle murmur of conversation filled the air.

JD ordered a cup of coffee and grabbed one for me as well. I sat across the table from the two women, trying to figure out what this was all about.

"What's with the disguise?" I asked.

"If anyone sees me talking to you..." She didn't want to finish the thought.

"Go on, tell him," Carolyn urged.

"Liam wasn't with me at the time of Bree's murder like I said."

"Where was he?" I asked.

She shrugged. "I don't know."

"But you two were at the party together?"

"I left early. I had a headache. He didn't get in until 4:30 or 5 AM."

I exchanged a glance with JD. Then I looked back to Elena. "Do you think he killed her?"

She didn't say anything.

"Why are you telling us this?"

In a cold and dispassionate voice, she said, "I caught the bastard cheating on me. I'm tired of covering for him."

"What motive would Liam have for killing Bree?"

There was another long silence.

She glanced around again, her nervous eyes darted from table to table, then scanned the street through the window.

The other patrons in the coffee shop went about their business chatting, snacking on desserts, clacking away on laptops. Nobody was interested in our conversation. At least, it didn't appear that way.

"Bree wasn't bankrupt," she said in a hushed tone.

She let that hang in the air for a long moment, drifting like a wisp of smoke.

"Liam had been embezzling funds from her for years. It started small, then he grew more brazen. Bad investments. Fake art."

A bell of recognition chimed in my brain.

"You saw the news about Vincent's death."

She nodded.

"Are you willing to testify?" I asked.

Her face twisted with fear. "Oh, no! Absolutely not."

I frowned. "Why not?"

"You have no idea the kind of people Liam is involved with."

"Who is he involved with?"

She glanced around again. Then the large sunglasses aimed back at me. "You need to be careful. I wasn't here. We never talked. And I will deny we had this conversation. I've already said too much."

She excused herself, then slipped out of the booth and quickly exited the coffee shop.

"Well, that was sort of, helpful," JD said, dryly.

"How did you find her?" I asked Carolyn.

"I'm persuasive and tenacious." Carolyn smiled. "I saw her at a club and approached her. I asked her to get in touch with me if she knew anything about Bree's death. I didn't expect to hear from her, then a day later, she called, and here we are."

"Nice work," I said.

"You'll also be pleased to know that I canvased the entire marina. I asked every yacht owner in the harbor if they saw anything. I kept detailed notes." She motioned to a spiral-bound notebook on the table.

"And?" I asked.

She shook her head. "Nobody saw anything. At least, nobody was willing to *say* they saw anything. But I'm not convinced. I met a woman who was hesitant and evasive. She seemed scared. I think she may be holding something back. I'll reach out to her again."

I took a sip of my coffee.

"Elena seemed pretty paranoid," I muttered.

"Wouldn't you be if your husband was a murderer?" Carolyn said.

"Just because he doesn't have an alibi doesn't make him a murderer," I said.

JD flashed me a sour look.

"Just playing devil's advocate," I said. "I don't think she was afraid of Liam. She was afraid of his associates. Who do you think they are?"

"From what I can tell, Liam has a lot of clients. And not all of them are aboveboard. I did some digging. One of his clients is a guy they call *Nails*. You might be able to find out more about him than I can. Word on the street is he is one of the largest traffickers in Europe."

"Drugs?" JD asked.

"Drugs and girls."

"Isn't he a film financier?" I asked.

Carolyn nodded. "He funds non-studio pictures in the $20-30 million range. Made mostly for foreign distribution. But the movies are just a way to move money around and launder money. His real business is the drugs and the girls. He brings aspiring actresses over from eastern bloc countries and passes them around to producers. The girls get bit parts in studio movies and get an H-1 visa in the United States. But they have to keep performing *extracurricular* activities, if you know what I mean, if they want to stay in the country. Otherwise their visa get's revoked."

I thought about things for a moment. "You need to be careful." You've been running around asking a lot of questions. Somebody already made an attempt on our lives. I think maybe it's time you head back to the States."

Her face tensed. "No. I'm not leaving until we get to the bottom of this."

"I don't think any of us are safe right now," I said.

"I can handle myself," Carolyn said with confidence. "Nothing you say is going to make me stop."

Carolyn wasn't afraid, and I realized I couldn't talk her out of anything.

"Do you think Liam killed Vincent?" Carolyn asked.

"I think Liam could have been working with Vincent. Bree bought the fake painting, and maybe Vincent split the profits with Liam? Who knows?"

"He sure seemed upset about the painting being fake. Maybe Liam got scared we might connect him with Vincent," JD said. "Maybe he was afraid Vincent would start talking?"

"Or maybe someone else found out Vincent was selling fakes," I suggested.

"I say we grab Liam and beat a confession out of him," JD said.

The idea was tempting. "This is all just conjecture. We need something concrete."

"Good idea. We'll put that bastard in cement shoes and drop him to the bottom of the ocean and see if he starts talking. If he drowns, I guess that means he's guilty." JD smiled.

"We need to get hard evidence, then present it to Inspector Géroux."

"Where's the fun in that?" JD asked.

My phone buzzed, interrupting the conversation.

It was Aria.

I figured I should answer. "Hey, what's going on?"

"I'm shocked," she said. "You actually answered."

"Sorry. It's been kind of crazy."

"I just wanted to call and see how you were doing?"

I excused myself and slid out of the booth. I stepped out of the coffee shop onto the sidewalk. "I'm okay. JD got shot. But he's fine."

Aria gasped. "What's going on?"

I filled her in on all the details.

"So, did you have a thing with Bree? It's all over the news." Aria said with a slight hint of jealousy in her voice. "I mean, I understand if you did."

I felt like I was walking into an ambush. "I thought we had an open thing going on?"

22

"We do," Aria said. "But that doesn't mean I'm not going to get a little jealous when you bang a hot movie star."

"Well, you don't have anything to be jealous about now," I said, dryly.

She huffed, not amused by my morbid sense of humor. "How long are you staying in Monaco?"

"Until I get this thing settled."

"I finished my modeling job in New York. Maybe I could hop on a plane. I feel really bad that I ditched you." She paused, changing direction. "You did use protection when you fucked her, didn't you?"

"Of course," I said.

"Good. 'Cause I heard she got around," she muttered.

There was an uncomfortable silence.

I don't know if Bree got around or not. I tended to take the gossip with a grain of salt. "I don't think you should come here."

"Oh," she said, dejected.

"Not until I get this sorted. It's too dangerous."

"Oh," she replied in a perkier tone.

"Listen, now is kind of a bad time. I'll call you soon."

"I guess I'll be around," she said in a sad, hesitant voice. "Take care of yourself."

"You too."

I hung up the phone and went back inside.

I didn't know what the hell was going on with our relationship, if you could call it that. It was sort of like a *friends with benefits* thing, but at the current time there weren't any benefits. And I didn't feel like thinking about it at the moment.

I slipped back into the booth beside JD.

"I'm going to go back to the marina," Carolyn said. "See what else I can dig up."

"We'll go with you," I said.

"That's not necessary."

"Yes, it is," I insisted.

Carolyn made a pouty face at me.

We left the coffee shop and strolled down to the Marina.

JD groaned occasionally, but he insisted that we keep walking instead of catching a cab. He said the exercise would be good for him. "Keeps the blood flowing. Promotes healing."

It was odd to hear something even remotely health-conscious come out of his mouth.

We followed Carolyn to a boat two slips down from the *Silver Screams.*

"Excuse me, is anyone on board?" Carolyn shouted.

A crew person emerged from the salon a few moments later.

The boat was a 90 footer. Modest in comparison to some of the other mega-yacht's, but it still looked like a floating palace.

Carolyn checked her spiral notebook. "I'm looking for Bianca Reshetkova. Is she aboard?"

"I'll check," the deckhand said.

He disappeared into the salon, and Bianca emerged a few moments later.

She had satiny brown hair and olive skin. She wore a black bikini with gold hoops connecting the fabric at the hips. There was lots of bling on her fingers.

Her face tensed, and she let out an exasperated sigh when she saw Carolyn. "I told you everything I know. I've got nothing more to say."

"I'd just like to ask a few more questions."

Bianca's brown eyes flicked to me and JD. A wave of recognition washed over her face. She must have recognized me from the news.

"Please, leave now! I didn't see anything. It's terrible what happened, but I can't be of assistance to you."

She glanced down the dock, to see if anyone had followed us.

"Bree Taylor was murdered," I said. "We know who did it. We just need some evidence." I pulled out my phone and searched the Internet for a picture of Liam. I found an image of him and his wife at a movie premiere. "Would you mind taking a look at this man and telling me if he looks familiar?"

The muscles in her jaw flexed. She took a deep breath and hesitantly made her way across the gangway.

I stood on the dock, holding out my phone so she could see the display.

She took a brief glance, and in the micro-second before she answered, I saw a hint of recognition in her eyes. "No. I'm sorry. I've never seen that man before in my life."

I smiled. "Thank you for your time. Sorry to bother you. Let me give you my number, in case you think of any details that might be helpful."

"I don't need your number. There are no other details to remember. Now, if you'll excuse me," she said, then spun around and hurried back into the salon.

"She's hiding something," JD said.

"That's exactly what I thought," Carolyn added.

"The slip next to Bree's boat was empty the night of her death. Bianca would have had an excellent view of the starboard side," I said.

We left the marina and headed back to the hotel. In the room, JD got a call from Madison, and the news wasn't good.

"What do you mean, she's gone?" JD's face filled with concern.

"I mean, she's not here," Madison said. Her voice filtered through the tiny speaker on JD's phone. "I had to run some errands, and when I got back, she was gone. Alejandro said he saw her get into a silver Honda and leave. She had a bag packed."

JD grimaced.

"Maybe she's just going to see a friend, or taking a change of clothes to go out after work? But I don't think she's working today," Madison said. "I feel terrible. I was supposed to be keeping an eye on her."

"I'll try calling her," JD said.

"I called a dozen times, and she hasn't answered," Madison said, frantic. "She won't respond to my texts."

JD tried to play it cool, but I could see that he was worried. "Let me know if you hear anything from her."

"I will. I'm so sorry, Jack."

JD hung up the phone.

"Scarlett?" I asked.

"That little miscreant has chosen the perfect time to go

AWOL," Jack said. "I swear to God if she gets herself in more trouble..."

He just shook his head.

"I'm sure she'll be okay," I said, trying to put a positive spin on it.

"She's got a court date in less than a month for possession. If she falls off the wagon and gets picked up again she's on her own."

JD looked like he was about to explode. "That just chaps my hide. She knows better. She is on lockdown, and she knows the only time that she is supposed to leave the house is to go to work. And she's supposed to come straight home. No screwing around. No drinking. No going out to clubs. I know she's got a fake ID. Hell, she's had one since she was 14. You would not believe the collection I have taken from her over the years."

"Who's Scarlett?" Carolyn asked.

"I'm beginning to wonder that myself," JD sighed.

JD gave Carolyn the backstory.

"Why don't you head back to the States," I said. "I can take care of things here."

"No," JD said. "Scarlett's an adult. If she wants to screw up her life, that's her choice."

"Maybe she's just going to visit a friend?" Carolyn suggested.

"All of her friends are little delinquents too."

Carolyn frowned.

There was a long moment of silence as JD processed the situation.

"I'm going to go back to my hotel room and look over my notes," Carolyn said. The tension in the room was thick, and it made her uncomfortable. "I'll see if there's anything I missed. I'll let you know if I turn up anything."

"I don't think it's safe for you to be wandering around by yourself right now," I said.

"Don't worry about me," Carolyn replied with a grin. She pulled a small subcompact pistol from her purse.

My eyes widened. "You know how to use that thing?"

"Absolutely."

"Why do I find this so concerning?" I asked with a healthy dose of sarcasm.

She rolled her eyes. "Just because Bree had a restraining order against me doesn't mean that I'm crazy."

JD arched a curious eyebrow. "It doesn't?"

Her wild eyes narrowed at him.

JD raised his hands in surrender. "Whatever you say. You've got the gun."

She tucked it back into her purse.

"I don't suppose you have a local license for that?" I asked.

"No. Are you going to turn me in?" she asked in a sassy tone.

"I'm just saying... If you get caught with that, you will be in big trouble."

"I'd rather be in trouble than dead," she said.

She had a point.

After Carolyn left the hotel room, JD muttered, "She's cute, but goddamn, that girl scares me."

23

J D fidgeted nervously. It was easy to see he had one thing on his mind—Scarlett.

The pain meds had long since worn off, and the day's activity had caught up with him. He fumbled for the bottle of pain pills, emptied several into his palm, and tossed them down the hatch, followed by a gulp of whiskey.

"Where the hell did I go wrong?" He groaned. "I've been a good dad. I provided a good environment. I put a roof over her head, food on the table, and tried to be a good role model. I'm not perfect, but who the hell is?"

"It's not your fault, JD. Kids experiment. Sometimes they take it too far. And these days, the consequences seem a little more intense. Life isn't as simple as it was when we were younger. And *certainly* not when you were younger."

His eyes narrowed at me.

"I mean, the only thing you had to worry about was not getting eaten by dinosaurs."

"Funny," he said flatly.

JD eased into a chair by the window. "When these pain pills kick in, we're going to get something to eat. I'm starving."

The sun was setting, and I figured it was time for a cocktail as well. I poured myself a drink and relaxed for a moment.

JD seemed to calm down after a few minutes.

I'd seen another Italian restaurant a few blocks over that looked interesting. We left the hotel and headed toward Bella Luna. It was an upscale casual eatery that overlooked the harbor. The mâtre d' seated us, and we ordered a round of drinks while we perused the menu.

I ordered the linguini with clam sauce, and JD ordered the lasagna. When they brought the steaming plates out, I regretted my decision. The linguine was awesome, don't get me wrong, but that lasagna looked, and smelled, amazing! The sauce, the meat, the gooey cheese... mmm.

JD didn't say much. His mind was back in Coconut Key. "I think I probably should head back home. That girl is going to be the death of me."

"I think that's a good call. You're going to drive yourself crazy if you stay here."

"I hate to leave you."

"I'm fine. Besides, I'm not the one who got shot."

"That was just bad luck."

We were halfway through the meal when I got a text from Carolyn. *[I have what we need].*

It was another cryptic message.

I texted: [What do you have?]

[You know I don't like sending sensitive information over text].

She had every reason to be paranoid. I knew exactly how fragile the average person's privacy was. Cobra Company violated it on a daily basis. So did the US government. Hell, there was a keyword searchable database of every phone conversation, text message, and email ever sent.

There was more data than the spooks knew what to do with.

But in the era of machine learning, threats and terrorist networks were more easily detected.

The thing that always frightened me about signals intelligence was that the government relied solely on externally developed software. There was no telling what backdoors were hidden in the code, or who had access?

[Meet me at my hotel room].

[Okay. We're just finishing dinner].

[Hurry. This is important].

I showed the text to JD who regarded it with a healthy dose of skepticism. "I'm telling you, that girl frightens me. What if she snaps and goes bat-shit crazy?"

"What is she going to go crazy about? I don't have a restraining order against her."

His eyes narrowed at me. "What if she fixates on you?"

"I don't think I'm her type."

JD scoffed. "Please, I've seen how well you do with the ladies. The rest of us are invisible when you're around. You could make a nun break her vows."

I modestly dismissed his comment.

We settled our tab and left the restaurant. We headed down *Rue Grimaldi*, then veered onto *Avenue d'Ostend* and made our way to the *Château Magnifique*.

It was a luxury five-star hotel that was a few minutes walk from the casino and *Larvotto Beach*.

Carolyn was loaded.

She had been living on a trust fund since her early 20s. With too much money, and too much time on her hands, and a compulsive personality, I began to see how she could fixate her attention on things of interest. She didn't have a job, didn't want for money, and until this point, had occupied her mind with the life of Bree Taylor.

The lobby was ornately decorated. There were marble floors, and a pianist tickled the keys of the grand piano. The furniture was elegant, and an interior waterfall trickled, making the lobby feel like a meditation chamber.

The gold crest of the hotel's *CM* logo was emblazoned on the black elevator doors. I pressed the call button, the doors slid open, and we stepped aboard the lift. At the fourth floor, I took a left down the hallway and knocked on room #415.

There was no answer.

I knocked again. "Carolyn. It's me. Tyson."

Still nothing.

I put my ear to the door and listened. The muffled sound of the TV barely filtered through the door.

I exchanged a wary glance with JD.

I knocked again. "Carolyn. Are you in there?"

24

J D stayed at the door while I ran down the hall, bursting into the stairwell and spiraling down to the lobby. I rushed to the desk clerk. "I'm concerned about my friend in #415. She won't answer."

"Maybe she stepped out," the clerk said with a thick French accent. "Or maybe she just doesn't want to see you."

"She just invited me over," I said, glaring at the man. "Can you open her door? I'd like to do a wellness check."

The clerk lifted a perturbed eyebrow. "Hold on. I will get the manager."

After wasting time explaining the scenario to him, he agreed. He escorted me up to the room, assuring me that everything was fine, and I was probably overreacting. He slid the card key into the lock, and the access light flashed green. He pressed the handle and pushed into the room and gasped at what he saw.

I rushed in through the open door to see Carolyn sprawled

out on the bed. Her skin was pale, and her eyes were fixed at the ceiling. She had no color in her lips.

I felt for a pulse on her wrist, but she didn't have one. Her skin was cold.

That sick feeling twisted my stomach. I should never have left her on her own.

She had a band tied around her left arm, and an empty syringe was on the bed—next to a spoon and a lighter.

I immediately started chest compressions, though I knew it was far too late. "Call emergency services! We need some narcan."

Narcan (Naloxone) was a drug that counteracted the effects of opiates.

The manager hesitated for a moment, dazed by the situation. Then he darted to the phone and called an ambulance.

I spent the next several minutes trying to revive Carolyn, pumping her chest to no avail. When the EMTs arrived, they took over and quickly pronounced her deceased.

JD and I looked around the hotel room, without disturbing anything. I knew that once the police arrived, we wouldn't have access to the scene any longer. From what I could tell, Carolyn's notebook was missing—the one with all of her notes and information she had gathered about Bree's murder.

Inspector Géroux arrived within a few minutes, and he wasn't particularly happy to see us. An exasperated sigh escaped his lips. "Why is it every time someone dies you are in close proximity?"

"I guess I'm just bad luck," I said.

He looked over the scene, and a forensics photographer snapped pictures.

"Was she a friend of yours?" Géroux asked.

"Something to that effect."

"I'm glad that you and I are not friends," he quipped, dryly. "It seems your friend has overdosed."

"I think that's what someone would like us to believe," I said.

"And who is this mysterious *someone*?"

I shrugged.

"What are you doing here?"

"She invited me to come over."

"Were you two lovers?"

I sneered at him. "No. We've been discussing Bree's death. I think she might have gained some insight into the crime. I believe that's why she was murdered."

The inspector stopped just short of an eye roll. "This is not a homicide, yet." He paused. "Tell me your theory."

I explained to him all the reasons why I thought Liam Gordon had motive, means, and opportunity to kill Bree.

"An interesting and creative theory, but impossible."

My face twisted with confusion. "Why impossible?"

"Liam has a solid alibi."

"No he doesn't. His wife told me she lied to cover for him."

"I know. He wasn't with his wife. He was with another woman during the time of Bree's murder."

"Who?" I asked.

"I am not in the business of keeping the gossip magazines supplied with dirt. I'm afraid that information will remain confidential. Suffice it to say, I checked his alibi, and I am satisfied with it."

"What about Vincent's murder?"

"Liam was in Cannes at the time. There are witnesses."

"And where is he now?" I asked, incredulous.

"That, I do not know." He paused. "It is not for me to decide, but I consider this to be an accidental overdose."

"I saw nothing to indicate that Carolyn was a user," I said.

"And how well did you know her?"

I didn't answer.

I didn't know her well at all.

"How much time have you spent with her?" Géroux asked.

"A few hours," I conceded, in a low mumble.

"And that is enough time to know a person's deep dark secrets?"

I said nothing and frowned.

"She could have been clean for months or years, then relapsed," Géroux said. "Stress can push some people over their limits. I see it happen all the time."

I couldn't argue with what he was saying. But I didn't like it. And I didn't buy it.

"We will know more once we have a full report from the medical examiner. Feel free to contact me if you would like additional information. In the meantime, I will politely ask you to leave while we continue our investigation." Inspector Géroux motioned for the door, and JD and I exited the suite.

I muttered to him in the hallway. "She didn't have any tracks on her arm."

"You never know. People get creative about places they shoot up."

I shook my head. "She hadn't been using."

JD shrugged. "How do you know that?"

"You don't seriously think she OD'd?" I asked, incredulous.

"No. I don't. But I've known people who've been pretty good at hiding their habits. And like the man said. You didn't know her very well."

"She didn't exhibit any signs of using."

We made our way back down to the lobby and exited the hotel. Blue lights flickered across the building from two parked police cars.

We caught a cab back to the Hôtel Impérial. As I climbed out of the car and stepped to the curb, a woman exited the cab behind us and approached. It took me a moment to place her face. Then I recognized her from the marina.

It was Bianca.

"Mr. Wild," she said, timidly. Her eyes gave a cautious glance around. "I need to speak with you. I was supposed to meet Carolyn at her hotel. But when I saw the police out front, I thought something dreadful had happened. She's not answering her phone. Then I saw you, and I followed you here."

A look of terror filled her eyes when I told her Carolyn was dead.

25

"Let's talk about this inside," I suggested.

In light of our previous attack, I didn't think discussing such matters on the street would be prudent.

Bianca readily agreed.

My eyes scanned for threats as we strolled back to our hotel room. I unlocked the door, made sure the room was clear, then invited Bianca in.

She looked dazed by the news of Carolyn's passing. "I can't believe she's gone. I just spoke with her."

"About Bree?"

"I told her the truth," Bianca admitted.

"So, you saw the murder?"

She nodded. "Yes, and I have it on video."

My eyes widened with surprise. I exchanged a glance with JD.

Bianca dug into her purse. "I recorded the whole thing on my phone."

She pulled out a smart phone and handed it to me after she unlocked the screen with her passcode. "The videos are in the photos app."

I scrolled through her phone and launched the video.

"I saw them that night. I'm almost embarrassed to admit it, but I was a little starstruck. That's why I took the video. I didn't have any idea what would happen next."

"And you told Carolyn you were bringing this to her?" I asked.

"Yes."

"Why not just go to the police?"

"No. No police. I don't want to get involved. That's why I didn't want to talk to you in the first place. I'll give you the video and you can do what you want with it. Then I'll delete it from my phone. I don't want to have anything to do with this."

Judging by the way people turned up dead, I didn't blame her.

I pressed play on the video, and what I saw threw me for a loop.

In crystal clear, ultra high definition footage, I watched Bree lean on the railing at the bow of her mega-yacht. Liam approached, and the two got into a heated discussion.

"I want my money back," Bree demanded. "All of it. Now."

Liam looked like he was in physical pain at the sound of the request. "I can't get it back now. I don't have it."

"Find it. You're a smart guy. Steal it from somebody else. But I want every last penny back."

"It's going to take time."

"Time is something you don't have. I'll go public with this. You'll be ruined."

A grim look washed over Liam's face. "You can't do that!"

"I can, and I will." Bree scowled at him. "I trusted you. I considered you a friend. How could you do this to me?"

Liam made a half-assed apology. "I'm sorry. I have a problem. I'm an addict. I couldn't control myself. I saw an opportunity, and I took it."

Bree rolled her eyes. "Don't give me that victim bullshit. You're a goddamn thief. Nothing more, nothing less."

Something off-screen drew their attention, and their heads turned.

Liam muttered, "I'll get your money. We'll discuss this later."

Savannah stumbled into the frame. A champagne bottle dangled from her fingertips, which was mostly empty at this point.

"Savannah, why are you still here?" Bree asked, disgusted.

She smiled and ran her fingers through Liam's hair. "Oh, just having a little fun."

Liam recoiled at her touch and slid out of reach.

Savannah's face crinkled up. "I'm not good enough for you now?"

Bree arched a curious eyebrow.

"Nothing happened," Liam assured.

Savanna scoffed. "I'll say. But it wasn't for lack of trying." Then she whispered, "He had a little performance anxiety. And when I say little, I mean *little*."

Liam scowled at her.

"And believe me, when this body can't do the trick, something is wrong." Savannah gave Liam a pathetic glance.

"She's lying," Liam said.

"What's the matter, worried your wife might find out?"

Bree seemed amused by the drama. "I think it's time you both left."

Savannah scoffed. "*Miss Fancy Pants* is too good for us."

"Nope. I'm just tired. And I don't like either one of you. So, take your skanky ass home."

Savannah's face tensed and turned red. Her eyes went crazy, and she swung the champagne bottle, back-handing it across Bree's face.

The bottle clanked as it hit her brow, echoing across the water.

The strike split a gash across her forehead and blood trickled down her face. The impact twisted Bree aside, and her momentum carried her over the railing. She tumbled overboard, splashing into the water.

Savanna gasped, her eyes wide, "Oh, shit!"

Bree floated facedown in the water, unconscious.

Liam stared at her, stunned.

"Do something!" Savannah growled.

There was a long pause and Liam thought about the situation. He glanced around the marina, but failed to see Bianca.

Savanna still clung onto the bottle, gripping it like a baseball bat. Liam grabbed her wrist and held it over the edge of the boat, making sure not to touch the bottle.

"What are you doing?" Savannah slurred.

"Let go!"

"What?"

"Let. Go."

Savannah complied, and the bottle splashed into the water. It bobbed a few times, turned on its side, then slowly sank.

The waves lapping against the hull of the boat kept pushing Bree against the shiny white surface, her head making a dull thump with each impact.

Liam took Savannah by the shoulders. "Listen to me. This didn't happen."

Savannah was hesitant.

"Your career will be over if this gets out. You understand me?

I'm just looking out for you. This is in your best interest. Trust me."

Savannah's eyes brimmed. Her frazzled expression gazed at Liam. "What will we say?"

"Let's get out of here. We'll talk about this later."

Liam ushered Savannah toward the stern. That's when the video ended.

26

The video was hard to watch. My throat tightened, and my fingers balled into fists.

I couldn't believe I hadn't heard the commotion? Then again, I hadn't slept in 48 hours and had overindulged in some fine whiskey. Perhaps it wasn't that surprising?

A knock at the door startled all of us. "Guest services."

I breathed a little easier and exchanged a glance with JD.

"It's probably the extra pillow I ordered this morning. How's that for service?" he said with an annoyed tone.

He moved to the door and pulled it open. As he did, a heavy foot kicked it the rest of the way. The door slammed into JD, and he slammed into the wall. In a flash, two men with guns stormed into the room and secured the area.

They were big guys with broad shoulders, square jaws, and tight haircuts. They wore all black. One was blond, the other brunette. The blond was a little taller, and a little thicker with muscle. They didn't have a friendly bone in their bodies.

"Give me the phone," the blond demanded.

I tossed it to him, throwing it just out of reach. It missed his fingertips and clattered to the floor.

"Whoops," I said.

He wasn't amused.

He aimed the pistol at Bianca and fired two suppressed rounds. The bullets snapped across the room and impacted her abdomen with a thud.

A look of terror washed over her face as blood blossomed on her blouse. She clutched her stomach and fell to the ground, writhing in agony.

"Still think this is a game?" the blond asked.

I shook my head.

"Back away and keep your hands in the air where I can see them."

I complied.

He squatted down, keeping his weapon aimed at me as he scooped the phone from the floor. He stood up and slipped it into his pocket. "Are there any other copies of the video?"

"No." I wondered how he knew about it? Had they been monitoring Carolyn's phone? "Who are you?"

"None of your fucking business." He waved the barrel of the pistol toward the door, motioning me to exit. "The boss would like to speak with you."

I exchanged a wary glance with JD, then looked back at the goon. "I'm kind of busy right now. How about a rain check?"

"I thought we were done playing games," Blondie said in a disappointed voice. He aimed the barrel of his pistol at JD.

"No," I yelped. "It seems my schedule's all cleared up."

"That's what I thought."

He put another bullet into Bianca before we left the hotel room. She had been groaning. All traces of life vanished with the third bullet.

The goons escorted us down the hall to the stairwell, and we spiraled our way down to the lobby.

"Don't try anything funny," the blond enforcer said.

I was all out of witty come-backs.

We slipped out of the back exit and were forced into a black SUV that waited in the alleyway. It smelled like stale cigarettes and the cheap cologne of the muscle-heads. It whisked us through the city, down to the harbor.

Blondie sat beside me in the backseat, along with JD. It was a large SUV, but three of us abreast made things a little too cozy. He kept his gun aimed at me the entire time.

So did the thug upfront.

I decided I'd take the ride and see where this was going.

At the marina, our wrists were zip-tied, and we loaded onto a Zodiac. It looked identical to the Combat Rubber Raiding Craft the Navy SEALS used. The engine roared, and we raced across the inky water, slipping into the night like we were on some type of clandestine mission. Only this time, I wasn't dashing off to save anyone—I needed saving.

The tender bounced across the waves, and mists of salt water splashed in my face. We skimmed through the harbor, leaving the mega-yachts behind, passing a cruise ship that was docked near the entrance.

Then we hit the open water.

The glimmering lights of Monaco became specs on the horizon as we disappeared into the night. We were more than a mile out when I saw the running lights on the horizon.

I felt somewhat relieved. For a moment, I thought they were going to take us deep out to sea, shoot us, and push us overboard. There was no telling where the current would take our bodies.

We approached a massive super-yacht. It was easily close to 200 feet. It was the pinnacle of luxury. Three decks and had accommodations for 10 to 12 people, I guessed.

The Zodiac pulled to the swim platform of *Stocks and Blondes*, and the goons ushered us aboard the yacht. There was a massive garage that stored the tender and other watercraft. It held a variety of aquatic toys—jet skis, wake-boards, you name it.

We climbed the steps to the aft deck where there was a lounge, a table, two coolers, and a retractable sunshade that was still deployed—even though it was well after sunset.

The goons pushed us into the salon which was luxuriously appointed. They shoved us onto a sofa that faced the stern. There was a fully stocked bar to port, and a gentleman standing behind it, mixing himself a drink. I recognized him from Bree's party.

Nails.

He looked to be mid 40s, dark hair, dark eyes and handsome, but rugged features. He'd been in a few fights back in his day as evidenced by the scar on his left brow. He was impeccably dressed with a bespoke suit from *Ungari*, or *Valentini*, if I had to guess. The *Hälfliger* watch on his wrist cost upwards of $50,000. Pocket change for a man of his stature.

Liam hovered near the bar, nervously. A mist of sweat beaded on his forehead. His wide eyes glanced about, and he swallowed hard as he saw us.

I scowled at the scumbags.

Blondie handed Bianca's cell phone to Nails. He tabbed through a few screens, launched the photos app, and began to watch the video.

A scowl twisted on his face. He turned the display to face Liam and showed him the gruesome video. "Maybe next time you can cover your tracks better. This is unacceptable."

Liam tried to defend himself. "How was I supposed to know that would happen? This is all Savannah's fault."

"You had problems long before Savannah. You should never have let yourself get into that situation," Nails chastised.

"You're right. I'm sorry."

"Your incompetence has threatened my entire operation. I've had to run around cleaning up after your mess. It's been a real headache. Despite my reputation, I don't like doing this type of thing."

"I know, I'm sorry," Liam said, his voice trembling.

"Do you know what kind of damage this video could cause if it got out?"

"I know," Liam said.

Nails returned his gaze to me. He stepped away from the bar and sauntered close, hovering over me. "And you have caused a great deal of trouble. You could have walked away at anytime, but no, you kept pushing."

"I guess I'm just stubborn."

A thin smile tugged at Nails's lips. "And stupid."

"Why do you care what happens to Liam?" I asked. "Why get involved?"

"Liam is very good at what he does. I have many business activities. Some legitimate, some not so legitimate. Liam takes the not so legitimate proceeds and makes them usable."

"He launders your money," I said.

"He makes it squeaky clean. He does a good job, and at a price that I find reasonable. I don't want to have to find a replacement. And there is a chance that if someone starts poking into Liam's business, it might expose my own. I don't like risk. I don't like exposure. Liam has put me at risk."

His eyes burned into Liam.

"How do you know that video hasn't been uploaded to the Internet?" I asked.

"I don't. But I'm guessing it hasn't. If that were the case, the authorities would be looking for Liam and Savannah Skye. I haven't heard anything about it on the Entertainment Network." He smiled. "And something tells me I'm not going to."

"Is this the part where you kill us and dump us overboard?" I asked.

"No. I'm not going to kill you." He paused for a long moment. "Liam is."

Liam's eyes widened, and he swallowed hard.

Nails looked at Liam. "Your mess. You clean it up."

Nails reached in his pocket and drew a pistol from a shoulder holster. It was a 9mm. He checked to make sure the weapon was on safe, then handed it to Liam.

The financial manager was hesitant to take it.

"Go ahead. Don't make me lose faith in you."

Liam stepped away from the bar and took the pistol.

"Have you ever shot a pistol before?" Nails asked, deriving some type of perverse pleasure from the whole scenario.

"No," Liam stammered.

"Well, this should be fun. All you need to do is aim and pull the trigger."

Liam looked at Nails expecting more instructions.

"What are you waiting for?"

Liam's frantic eyes glanced back to the weapon.

"Start with the burnout. I want Mr. Wild to see his friend die before him."

JD's face crinkled. "Who are you calling a burnout?"

Nails seemed to admire JD's defiance.

Liam staggered toward the sofa and stood in front of JD. He had bad form and worse trigger control. His finger was wrapped around the trigger before he even took aim. Liam held the gun out, pointing it at JD's chest. The pistol rattled in his hand. The safety was still on, but Liam seemed oblivious. He shied away, anticipating the loud bang and recoil of the weapon.

It would have been funny if we weren't on the business end of the barrel.

27

"Not in the salon!" Nails shouted.

Liam swallowed again, then glanced across the salon at his boss. "Sorry."

"I prefer not to have bloodstains on my sofa, or my deck."

"Where should I do it?" Liam stammered.

Nails rolled his eyes.

He explained like he was speaking to a child. "Take him aft and position him against the gunwale. Then, when you blow his head off, hopefully he falls overboard. When you're done, swab the deck with bleach to get rid of the stains."

Blondie grabbed JD by the collar and dragged him out of the salon, into the cockpit.

Liam followed.

I gritted my teeth and clenched my fists. My heart pounded in my chest as I struggled against the zip-tie, then I remembered the lighter in my pocket. I dug my fingers into my back pocket and fished out the gold lighter that belonged to Katya.

Liam put the pistol to JD's head. "Are you sure you want to do this? You're gonna have to live with this the rest of your life."

Liam hesitated.

"Do it!" Nails shouted.

Liam took aim, steadied his resolve, and squeezed the trigger.

Nothing happened.

The safety was still on.

"Take off the safety, you idiot!" Nails growled.

Liam flipped the safety selector switch, swallowed again, then took aim.

I managed to strike the flint and spark a flame which quickly melted through the plastic zip-tie—and some of my skin, unfortunately.

Blondie hovered behind the sofa, to my left. I grabbed Blondie's gun, jammed an elbow into his groin, and stripped the weapon from him as he doubled over.

I double tapped two shots into Liam before he could pull the trigger. Muzzle flash flickered, and smoke wafted from the barrel. Brass shell casings spiraled from the ejection port, and the recoil hammered against my palm.

I won't lie, it felt good.

The bullets raced through the salon and drilled into Liam's

chest. Geysers of blood spewed from the wounds. His face filled with a look of utter disbelief as he tumbled back and fell on top of the garage and slid down to the swim platform.

I heard his body splash into the water.

I spun the weapon around and blasted several shots at Nails as he reached for a shotgun behind the bar.

My first shot missed.

The other tagged him in the shoulder, spinning him around.

Glass shattered, and bottles of whiskey broke, filling the compartment with the smell of single malt scotch, mixed with the sharp scent of gunpowder.

Nails groaned in agony as he writhed on the floor.

Blondie leapt over the couch and tackled me. We crashed into the glass coffee table, showering razor-like shards across the deck.

The gun clattered away, sliding onto the aft deck.

The big bastard was on top of me. He cocked his fist back and hammered it into my face.

His meaty fist felt like a wrecking ball.

The impact twisted my head to the side, mashing my cheek into the deck. Several shards of glass embedded into my skin. He kept pummeling me, tenderizing my cheek, grinding the soft flesh against my teeth.

The tinny metallic taste of blood filled my mouth.

I finally managed to buck the behemoth off me. I rolled

aside and staggered to my feet, and we squared off against each other.

The ogre charged me.

I tried to sidestep, but the bastard was quick for a big guy.

He grabbed me with one arm and slung me to the deck like I was nothing.

More shards of glass embedded into my skin.

I coughed as the wind was knocked out of my lungs.

The big ogre planted a knee on my chest and went full tilt on my face. His fist kept hammering down like a giant cinderblock.

Things got worse when he reached for a long shard of glass that resembled a kitchen knife. He grabbed it and stabbed down, the point of the shard angling toward my throat.

I managed to grab his wrist, blocking the blow.

The veins in my neck bulged as I struggled against his strong forearm. The glass blade quivered as he drove it closer and closer toward my jugular.

This was a losing battle.

The point drew precariously close to my skin.

JD squirmed on the deck near the stern with his wrists tied behind his back. He fumbled for the gun.

He managed to grasp it and twist around just as the shard was about to pierce my flesh. He angled the gun behind his back and squeezed the trigger.

BAM!

Muzzle flash lit up the night air, and smoke wafted from the barrel.

The bullet rocketed across the salon and smacked into the goon's rib cage.

It knocked him off me, and the shard shattered as it fell to the deck beside my face.

I spun free and sprang to my feet.

Blondie tried to get up, but fell back down. His labored breaths gurgled as blood filled his lungs. He looked at me with horrified eyes, and his massive hands clutched the sucking wound in his chest.

He couldn't stop the flow of blood seeping between his fingers. Blondie died like a fish flopping on the deck, gasping for air.

I sprinted to the aft deck and used my lucky lighter to burn through the zip-ties that bound JD's wrists. "Holy shit, dude! Did you even aim that thing?"

"I hit the target, didn't I?"

"You could have missed and shot me!"

"Ungrateful little prick. You'd have been dead in another second."

I helped JD to his feet. "Thanks."

"You could sound a little more excited about it."

"I'm excited. This is my excited face," I said, staring at him flatly.

JD sneered at me.

We moved back into the salon. Nails groaned behind the bar as he writhed on the deck in agony.

JD fired two shots into the dirtbag. "Whoops. Accidental discharge."

I grabbed Bianca's phone from the bar counter, and JD and I decided it was best if we vacated the vessel, pronto.

We moved down to the swim platform and climbed aboard the tender. We cast off the lines, and I started the outboard motor. With a twist of the throttle, we banked around and headed back toward Monaco.

We tossed the pistols into the water along the way. Getting caught with a weapon that was responsible for multiple deaths didn't seem like a good idea.

There were several crew members left aboard *Stocks and Blondes*. They were smart and stayed below deck. They didn't involve themselves in Nails's business. Working for the mob, you learned to keep your head down. See nothing and say nothing. The less you know the better.

The Zodiac whined as I kept the throttle on full, heading back to the harbor.

We pulled to the dock and climbed out of the boat. I set it adrift in the harbor, and we hobbled back toward the hotel.

I had cuts and scrapes all over my face, arms, and back. The square metal tubing that made the framework of the coffee table had done a number on my back when Blondie and I crashed into it. It hurt like hell, and I knew I was going to feel it in the morning.

The police were waiting for us when we returned to the hotel. We were surrounded the minute we stepped into the lobby, and cold steel handcuffs slapped around our wrists.

With Bianca's dead body in our hotel room, I had some explaining to do. I wasn't too worried about it. I had the video evidence of Bree's murder and figured I could talk my way out of this.

They stuffed us in the back of a police car and weren't too gentle about it. JD and I both groaned. All I could think about was stealing a few pain pills from him.

At the station, we were put into an interrogation room and our personal effects were confiscated. I had Bianca's phone in my pocket and they took that as well as my own.

We sat in the interrogation room for half an hour. The plain room with dingy white walls and brilliant fluorescent lighting was enough to drive a person mad.

Inspector Géroux finally entered and took a seat at the table opposite JD and me. "The hotel recently installed security cameras in the alley and around the premises. I have reviewed the footage and saw that you were kidnapped. I'm assuming the men who took you were responsible for the death of Bianca Reshetkova?"

"You would be correct," I said.

"I also saw the video on Carolyn's phone. It seems I owe you an apology. You were correct to think that Bree's death was not an accident."

I tried not to smile, but I wasn't doing a very good job. "You mind doing something about these handcuffs."

"Certainly."

Géroux stood up and strolled around the table. He dug into his pocket, fumbled for a key, then released the cuffs from around my wrist.

He did the same for JD.

I rubbed my wrists as the tight cuffs had carved grooves into my skin.

"A warrant has been issued for the arrest of Savannah Skye, along with Liam Gordon."

I hesitated for a moment, debating whether to tell him he didn't need to bother looking for Liam. I figured we'd cross that bridge when we came to it.

"Are we free to go?" I asked.

Inspector Géroux nodded.

I pushed away from the table and stood up. I shook hands with the Inspector on the way out.

"Once again, I apologize for the inconvenience," Géroux said.

We left the jail and caught a cab back to the hotel. Management had moved us into a new room. Once we got situated, I popped a few of JD's pain pills, and he took a handful as well.

The bottle was getting dangerously close to empty.

I washed them down with a glass of whiskey then took a shower. The water stung as it hit the lacerations on my skin.

28

W hen I woke the next morning, it felt like someone had stabbed a knife into my lower back—piercing pain that radiated down my left leg.

My whole body was tight.

It took a moment before I could move. I peeled my eyes open and wiped the sleep away as the morning light blasted into the hotel room. A freight train would have done less damage. I made a mental note to stop getting into fights with guys bigger than me.

It was wishful thinking.

I sat up on the edge of the bed and hovered there a moment, stretching and groaning, trying to get my blood flowing again.

I had the inclination to pop another pain pill, but I abstained. There was no point in going down that route. The last thing I needed was an opioid addiction.

I stood up, stretched, and staggered to the bathroom. I figured a hot shower would loosen things up, and it did, somewhat.

My phone rang when I got out of the shower. The caller ID read: *Joel Agent*.

"Have you seen?"

"Seen what?"

"Turn on the news."

I turned on the TV and got dressed. JD was pulling himself out of bed and didn't look pleased about it.

To my shock, Savannah Skye had been apprehended, and was in custody.

The broadcast was in French, but I was fluent. A reporter interviewed Inspector Géroux. "This morning Savannah Skye was apprehended in connection with the death of Bree Taylor. There is incontrovertible evidence to suggest Ms. Skye is responsible, along with a co-conspirator."

Several other reporters shouted questions, but Inspector Géroux ignored them.

Géroux continued, "This new evidence would not have come to our attention without the assistance of Tyson Wild, and I would like to take this opportunity to state publicly he is no longer a person of interest."

"What about my contribution?" JD griped.

"I'm sure he just forgot," I said with a grin.

"You'd still be in jail if it wasn't for me," JD said with a playful scowl.

The news broadcast cut to footage of Savannah's arrest. The look on her face was priceless. All of her hopes and dreams were going up in flames. It couldn't have happened to a nicer person.

Video of Bree's murder had leaked to the press, and they aired a highly edited clip.

"This is going to be great for your career," Joel said, his excited voice filtering through the tiny speaker in my phone.

I rolled my eyes. "I really don't care about a career."

"You will when you see the first paycheck. Oh, by the way, I've got the tickets to the Grand Prix, courtesy of Susan."

"JD's flying out today. He's got some family issues back home."

"I'm sorry to hear that. You're going to stay, right? I'd like to set up a few more meetings."

I hesitated.

"It will be worth your while."

"I'll think about it."

"I gave Bree's sister your number. She's going to call you to express her gratitude." Joel could barely contain his excitement. "Get ready for a wild ride. We'll talk soon!"

I hung up and waited for JD to shower and get dressed, then we headed down for breakfast. There were pancakes, blueberry waffles, eggs, bacon, hash browns, and fresh coffee. Somehow it tasted better than usual.

In the back of my mind, I worried about reprisals from

Nails's organization. I wasn't sure if he was the big man on the totem pole, or a mid-level boss? If the latter, there would be someone above him who was angry that a good earner had been put out to pasture. But I was no stranger to having angry people gunning for me.

After breakfast, JD gathered his bags, and I saw him off as he took a cab to the heliport, then transferred to Nice. It was a long flight home, and he was worried sick about Scarlett—even though he pretended not to be.

The streets of Monaco echoed with the roar of race cars as they snaked their way through hairpin turns on the first day of *Free Practice*. It was Thursday. *Qualifying* was on Saturday, and the race was on Sunday.

I figured a few more days in Monaco wouldn't kill me. And I had to admit, I was looking forward to watching the Grand Prix.

That afternoon, I heard from Bree's sister, Willow. "I hope you don't mind me calling. I got your number from Joel."

"He mentioned you'd be getting in touch."

"I just wanted to thank you for everything that you've done."

"I'm just glad the truth came to light."

"Do you have a chance to meet for coffee?"

"Sure," I said.

"There's a great little beanery on the corner of *Avenue du Port* and *Rue Grimaldi*."

"I know the place."

"Let's say 4:30 PM?"

"Perfect."

I had never seen Willow before, but it wasn't hard to pick her out of the crowd. She had a striking resemblance to Bree, though not quite as glamorous.

She seemed shy and unassuming. She didn't command attention, and I assume that was largely by choice. She wasn't wearing high-end designer fashions, and she didn't look like she was about to step onto the red carpet.

She spotted me right away as I stepped into the coffee shop. "Tyson?"

I smiled and greeted her with a hug.

"I recognized you from the TV." She smiled. "Thanks for coming."

We ordered our drinks and took a seat at a table on the sidewalk. It was a nice afternoon. Blue skies with a few harmless clouds. A cool breeze blew through the streets. The city was relatively quiet in between practice sessions.

"Bree's death would have haunted me for the rest of my life if I hadn't known what truly happened," Willow said. "I am forever indebted to you for that."

"I needed closure myself."

"Were you two close?" Willow asked with a quizzical look on her face. "She hadn't mentioned you before."

"We'd just met. But, I think had we gotten to know each other better, we would have been great friends."

"Bree could just hit it off with some people," Willow said. "People were drawn to her. Obviously. But she just had that thing about her." Her eyes teared up. She casually wiped them away. "I don't have that."

I smiled. "Oh, don't sell yourself short."

"She always was the outgoing one. She never met a stranger," Willow said. "I, on the other hand, am perfectly content to mind my own business and stay home with a good book."

We chatted for a little while, and I think Willow needed to connect with me on some level. I was the last person to really spend any time with her sister. And getting to know me was perhaps a way of understanding what the last moments of Bree's life were about.

"I won't take up any more of your time," Willow said. "But you have my number. Please keep in touch. If there's ever anything I can do for you, please let me know."

She thanked me again, and we hugged before she left. Her eyes were teary again, and she wiped them dry and flashed a smile before turning away.

I watched her go and hoped that she would find a way to process her grief. I knew from experience that it was a long process. It doesn't seem real when it first happens. You feel like it's happening to someone else.

When my parents were murdered, I had the overwhelming feeling that they were still around, just out of sight. It took a long time for reality to actually sink in. You never get over the loss of a loved one, you just learn to deal with it. To put it in its proper place. To be grateful for the time you shared, but not be crippled by the loss.

Over the next few days I watched the qualifying sessions

and enjoyed a VIP Paddock Club pass. The tickets to this exclusive club cost €6000 each. The studio handed them out like they were candy.

The VIP Terrace was filled with the glitterati, drinking champagne, snacking on hors d'oeuvres, gossiping, and making deals. There were flat-screen displays that showed the action from multiple angles.

I got to stroll around pit-lane and see the cars up close and talk to some of the drivers.

Joel introduced me to several famous directors and producers. It was more of a networking event for him than anything else.

On race day, I leaned against the railing and watched from the terrace as the race cars tore up the track.

"You lied to me," a stunning brunette said in a thick French accent as she leaned against the railing next to me.

I'd recognize that velvety voice anywhere.

Katya lowered her sunglasses and arched an eyebrow at me.

"I didn't lie to you," I said.

"You're not a killer."

I shrugged. "There's a few people who might argue with that."

She huffed, mildly annoyed. "And I thought I had a story to tell."

"You still have a story to tell."

"It was so much more interesting when you were Bree's killer."

"Sorry to disappoint."

She reached into her purse and pulled out a cigarette. She stuck it between her red lips and fumbled for a lighter.

"I'm not sure you can smoke here."

"They can sue me."

I pulled the gold diamond studded lighter from my pocket and struck it. The flame flickered at the end of her cigarette, and she sucked in a deep breath, then blew out a steady cloud.

"Now you are my accomplice in crime." Her eyes widened. "My lighter. Where did you find it?"

"In the casino."

She snatched it from my hand. "See. These are my initials, *K.T.*"

"I see."

Her eyes narrowed at me, suspiciously. "Are you sure you didn't steal this from me when you were at my apartment?"

I laughed and raised my hands innocently, "I'm positive."

Her suspicious gaze lingered.

"It did save my life, however."

Her curious eyebrow lifted. "How so?"

I told her the story.

She handed the lighter back to me. "Then you should keep it as a souvenir."

"How would you ever light your cigarettes?" I asked in a sardonic tone.

"There will always be someone to light my fire." Her sultry eyes smoldered.

29

K atya wasn't lying. A woman like that would always have men falling all over themselves to do her bidding. I must admit, I did light her cigarette a few more times. Once after we tumbled around the sheets in her apartment again.

I wasn't big on dating women who smoked. It was usually like kissing an ashtray, but she kept her breath clean, and she always had a stick of gum handy in case of emergency. For her, I was willing to make an exception.

She had such elegant curves that I found myself more than willing to take a few laps around the track.

I didn't have a solid departure date. It was tempting to stay in Monaco and see just how long it would take me to die of Katya's secondhand smoke.

We were enjoying each other's company, but she was an incessant socialite. Out every night at all the parties and bars. She had to see and be seen. I'm not quite sure where her money came from, and I didn't want to know, but she was loaded. It was nothing for her to drop $2500 for a bottle of champagne at a bar.

As much fun as I was having, I decided it was time to head home.

The Grand Prix was over. The festival in Cannes was all wrapped up. All the LA transplants had gone back home. The city was quiet, and less crowded. I'm sure the locals breathed a sigh of relief that their small oasis was returning to normal.

I called JD and asked if he'd heard anything from Scarlett.

"She is definitely on my shit list," JD said. "After three days of not returning my texts and calls, she tells me she's okay. She went on a road trip with Sadie up to New York. I'm thinking maybe you could call Aria and see if she could look in on them?"

"Sure thing," I said. "You think she's full of shit? Is she really in NY?"

"I know she's full of shit. But I made her text me a picture from Manhattan. So, at least I know she's there. I made her send me a photo of her and Sadie in Times Square."

"What about her court date?"

"I told her if she misses it, that's it. She's cut off. No more funds from Daddy to cover legal fees."

I hung up with JD and called Aria. She was a little cold at first, but warmed up quickly. She said Scarlett had contacted her. She offered to let the girls stay at her place while they were in town. I decided to go to New York to make sure they stayed out of trouble. I was determined to see Scarlett back to Coconut Key in time for her court date.

I said goodbye to Katya, and she told me I was welcome in Monaco at any time.

I couldn't help but feel a little sad as I boarded the plane, and I couldn't get Bree out of my mind during the flight home. It would be strange to watch her next movie that was due for release soon. She had wrapped filming a few weeks before her death.

I didn't know if I could watch it.

I caught the 9:40 AM flight from Nice, and with one stop, I landed at LaGuardia at 4:54 PM local time. It was mid 70s and overcast. Thick gray clouds blanketed the sky, and a light rain drizzled.

The flight attendants waved goodbye as I exited the plane, and I walked up the jetway to the terminal. I felt a wave of familiarity wash over me—I wasn't home, but I was back in the United States. And it felt good. The south of France is great, but there is nothing like the good 'ole US of A.

The terminal was still under construction, but at least I didn't have to take a shuttle bus to get to *Ground Transportation* anymore.

I hopped into a black town car and we drove toward Manhattan. Aria lived on the upper East Side on 72nd Street. I marveled at the towering skyscrapers as we crossed the Triborough Bridge—and yes, I'm old-school, I'm always going to call it the Triborough. They spent $4 million to change the name to RFK, and replaced 139 signs, to honor the former Senator. Did the taxpayers really benefit from that?

The cabdriver took FDR down to East 71st Street, and we looped around 1st Avenue to 72nd. The East Gardens Plaza was a modern high-rise condominium that offered a host of resort like amenities—24-hour concierge, doorman, porters, on-site valet. There was a fitness center, an Olympic size indoor pool, hot tubs, sauna, steam room, and indoor squash and basketball courts.

I pushed into the lobby and strolled to the bank of elevators. I had never been to Aria's apartment before. At the 29th floor, I found apartment G and knocked on the door. I heard the girls' voices inside, then Aria called through the door, "Who is it?"

"Pizza delivery."

The light coming through the peep-hole flickered as she looked through it.

"I don't see a pizza box, Mister," she said, playfully.

"It's right here. It's got extra sausage."

She laughed at my crude joke and pulled open the door. Her arms wrapped around me, and her full lips kissed my cheek. She took my hand and pulled me into the apartment. "Well, this is it. What do you think?"

"Not too shabby," I said, glancing around.

The apartment had breathtaking views of the city. In the southwest corner of the apartment, her large terrace over-looked the East River, the skyscrapers of Midtown, the

Hospital for Special Surgery, and the Queensboro Bridge in the distance.

The 2 bedroom apartment was 1000 ft.² and cost $1.8 million. There was a $1500 monthly maintenance fee, and around $1700 in monthly taxes on top of the mortgage.

I guess being a famous Insta-model paid off?

The kitchen flowed into the living room with an open architecture. The corner terrace featured wood decking and balustrade panels, offering a sweeping view. The apartment had wide-plank hardwood floors that were stained in a dark rosewood. The kitchen had quartz countertops, and a spacious center island. The kitchen was loaded with state-of-the-art stainless steel appliances.

There were two bedrooms split on opposite sides of the living room. Scarlett and her friend, Sadie, stayed in the guest room. The master bedroom had a private en suite, and the guest bathroom was easily accessible from the main area or the guest suite.

Scarlett gave me a sheepish look as she approached for a hug. She knew what kind of trouble she was in.

I arched a stern eyebrow at her.

"I know, I know," she said, wrapping her arms around me.

"You can't run off like this."

"I just needed to get away for a little while. I've been so stressed out. And Aria was kind enough to let us stay." Scarlett smiled.

Aria raised her hands, innocently. "I had nothing to do with this. She was already in New York when she called me."

"Aria has been super cool," Scarlett said. "She set up a meeting with her agent, and she's been giving me the scoop on the whole modeling thing."

Scarlett introduced her friend, Sadie. One look, and I could tell she was trouble.

She had pink shoulder length hair, dark mascara, and creamy skin. The 19-year-old wore an oversized anarchy T-shirt that had been cut into a fashionable dress that hung off one shoulder. The belt around her waist showed off her petite figure, and the hem of her *dress* barely extended to her thighs. She wore black stilettos that accentuated her toned calves. She was ready for an evening on the town.

We shook hands and exchanged pleasantries.

"Don't be mad at Scarlett," Sadie said with a smirk. "This was all my idea. I'm the bad influence."

"You don't have to convince me of that."

She chuckled. "You don't understand. This was a once-in-a-lifetime opportunity. DPR is playing their last show ever at the *Garden* tonight?"

"DPR?"

"Dope Pilot Revolution," Sadie said.

"Oh, right. Those guys are assholes," I muttered.

Scarlett lifted a curious brow. "You know them?"

"I know the guitar player, Zazzle."

Both of their eyes brightened.

"Really, that's so cool!" Sadie said. She stepped closer and grabbed my arm. "Can you get us backstage?"

"Sorry. I'm not that cool."

"I don't know. You dated Bree Taylor. That makes you pretty cool in my book."

I could feel Aria's eyes blaze into me. I shrugged innocently. "I wouldn't call it dating."

Aria cleared her throat. "Next subject."

Sadie flashed her an apologetic glance.

"So, after the concert, you two are heading back home?" I asked, phrasing it as a subtle demand.

"After the meeting with Aria's agent," Scarlett said.

"When's that?"

"Tuesday afternoon," she said, sheepishly.

"And your court date is Thursday," I said.

"Plenty of time." Scarlett made a sad, pouty face. The one that she knew would get her everything she ever wanted. Then she laid on the high drama. "This could be my last moment of freedom. They could lock me up in some maximum-security prison for, like, the next 30 years. I could be put with hardened criminals. I'll be forced to join a gang to survive. I might have to do hits in the yard, stabbing other inmates with a shank to please my gang overlords. Then, I'll get life. This may be the last concert I ever see as a free woman."

I rolled my eyes. "This is your first offense. You're going to get a slap on the wrist, and a heavy fine."

"See. It's no big deal," she said, flippantly.

My eyes narrowed at her. "Oh, believe me, it's a big deal."

Scarlett smiled. "Great. So we're in agreement. It is a big deal, and I should enjoy this moment to the fullest."

There was no way to win an argument with this girl.

"I told JD I would have you back in time. You realize you're about *this* close to giving him a heart attack," I said with my thumb and index finger less than a millimeter apart.

"Sorry," Scarlett said with that adorable pouty face again.

I paused for a long moment, then sighed. "You can go to the concert. But I'm coming with you. And you two are not getting out of my sight for the duration of your stay here. As soon as your meeting is done with Aria's agent, I'm putting you on a plane, and we're going back to Coconut Key. Are we clear?"

She nodded with a mischievous grin. The two little delinquents exchanged a glance.

"You know the concert is sold out, right?" Sadie asked.

"No worries," Aria said. "I know a guy who can get tickets. Might have to pay a little more, but..."

I gave her a nod that I didn't mind paying a little extra. I mean, how much could it be?

Aria dialed her phone and got her connection on the line. "Hey, Brad. Do you have anything for tonight's show?"

30

Brad's thin voice crackled through the speaker in her phone. It wasn't quite loud enough for me to hear.

"He's got floor seats," Aria said. "Section C, to the right of the stage."

I nodded.

"No way!" Scarlett said, her eyes wide with envy. "We are in section 221, up in the nosebleeds. You can't have better seats than we do. That's not fair."

"How many do you have?" Aria asked Brad. She listened for a moment. "He's got four seats."

"Please, please, please!" Scarlett begged.

I gave a nod to Aria.

"We'll take them. How much?"

Brad's thin voice crackled back.

Aria covered the phone. "He wants $650 each. Face value is $475."

My jaw dropped. "Are you sure they're real?"

Aria nodded. "I've purchased dozens of tickets from him." Then she uncovered the phone. "We'll take them."

Both the girls cheered with joy.

I wondered who the hell was gonna pay for these?

I definitely owed JD one. But I didn't have $2600 cash on me.

Aria must have read my look. "Don't worry about it. I got it."

The girls hugged Aria, thanking her profusely. They bounced up and down and screamed, elated.

I couldn't believe we were paying that much to go see Zazzle's band.

"Brad's going to meet us at the venue and give us the tickets," Aria said after she hung up the phone.

The doors opened at 7:30 PM, and the first act went on at 9 PM. We ordered a pizza, then headed to the *Garden*.

We dumped the crappy tickets for face value near the venue, and Aria pocketed the cash. Fortunately, we didn't get caught. You had to be licensed and bonded to re-sell tickets in New York, and it was illegal to sell within 1500 feet of the venue.

The opening act was the *Loud Assholes*, and they were aptly named. I'd heard catfights that were more melodic. Screaming vocals and fast beats. Sloppy, angry guitar riffs that all sounded derivative. Maybe I was just getting old, but I couldn't decipher a single lyric.

As bad as the *Loud Assholes* were, *Dope Pilot Revolution* made my skin crawl. They had a few songs that I liked, but my encounter with Zazzle killed any enthusiasm I had for the band.

It was just bizarre. A week earlier, I had almost gotten into a fight with him on a yacht in Monaco. I thought life would begin to seem less surreal once I got back to the United States, but the strange drama of my life kept unfolding.

The seats were great. *For $650 apiece, they ought to be!* We were on the 2nd row of section C. I could spit and hit the stage—and I thought about it a few times.

The crowd roared when DPR went on. The bass drum boomed like a howitzer, and when Zazzle hit a power chord it growled like a chainsaw. Colored lights slashed the hazy air, and the lead singer screamed, "Hello, New York!"

The crowd erupted again.

In the old days, the arena would take on the sweet aroma of cannabis the minute the band took the stage. Now, everyone mostly vaped, but there were a few tokers here and there. Security didn't seem too uptight about it.

Scarlett and Sadie loved the show. They bounced up and down and sang the lyrics with their hands in the air. They disappeared a few times to *supposedly* use the restroom, but I know they went off to get high. They returned with tall cups of beer in their hands as well. I knew Scarlett had a fake ID, but the vendors weren't being too picky about who they served.

I quickly realized I was not cut out for the chaperone thing.

"Relax, let them have fun," Aria shouted in my ear, grabbing my arm and snuggling close. She could easily read the tension on my face.

"I'm supposed to be keeping her out of trouble."

"They're having harmless fun," Aria said. "You were that age once, remember?"

I arched an eyebrow at her.

"Loosen up. Have a little fun," she shouted over the noise.

I forced a smile. "You want anything to drink?"

"I'll take a Jack and Coke," she said.

I squeezed down the row, stepped into the aisle, and made my way to the vending area. The line wasn't too bad, but I wasn't too thrilled about paying $15 a pop for watered-down mixed drinks. I decided it was best to make them doubles (which doubled the cost). I bought two for each of us. I carried $120 worth of drinks back on a cardboard drink tray, praying someone didn't bump into me.

Somehow, I managed to make it back to my seat without spilling them. Aria took her drinks and kissed me on the cheek.

I tried to pretend I had never met Zazzle. I had to admit, the guy could shred on guitar. I managed to let my animosity go, and I enjoyed the show as best I could. The girls were happy, and that's all that really mattered.

My ears rang after the show like I had been in a prolonged gun battle, despite wearing earplugs.

The VIP seats we purchased came with backstage passes that included a *meet and greet*. The girls were ecstatic at the prospect of meeting the band. I doubted Zazzle would even remember me. He was pretty inebriated at the time, and it seemed like ancient history now.

The *meet and greet* was nothing more than the VIP ticket holders standing in a backstage hallway for 20 minutes, waiting for the band to come out of their dressing room. The band moved through the line quickly, shaking hands, and inviting pretty girls back to their hotel to party.

Zazzle instantly homed in on Scarlett and Sadie. He was shirtless, drenched in sweat, and that stringy black hair concealed most of his face. "You definitely have to come party with us!"

The girls' faces lit up.

"Absolutely!" Sadie replied.

"I don't think they'll be joining you," I interjected.

The girls' faces fell flat.

I felt like that stodgy old man. This was not a role that I wanted to take on.

Zazzle's face crinkled, and he brushed aside his greasy hair. He twisted to face me and almost lost his balance. "I know you. Still a dick, I see."

I gritted my teeth and forced a smile.

Zazzle turned back to the girls. "Lose the loser, and come with us."

Sadie grabbed his hand. "Ok. Sounds fun." Her sassy eyes found me. "Sorry, but you can't tell me what to do."

She followed her statement with a smile that said *fuck you,* then she grabbed Scarlett's hand and pulled her down the hallway with Zazzle.

I had completely lost control of the situation.

Scarlett looked at me and shrugged innocently as she shuffled away. "I promise, we won't get out of hand."

I clenched my jaw, and my face turned red.

"You want me to go with them?" Aria asked.

31

"Jack is right," I said. "It's not my job to keep her from making bad decisions."

"I'm sure she'll be fine," Aria said. "I've partied with several rock stars before. They're usually pretty tame... I mean, this isn't the 70s."

She tried to downplay the situation.

I watched Scarlett and Sadie disappear down the hallway with several other groupies.

"JD's going to kill me if anything happens to her."

"I'll go and keep an eye on them."

"No." I tried to convince myself that it was no big deal. "Harmless fun with rock stars, right?"

"Right," Aria agreed.

Neither one of us really believed it.

"They're adults."

"Right."

I still wasn't convinced.

"We should make use of the time. We have the apartment all to ourselves," Aria said with a naughty glimmer in her eyes.

I hesitated and glanced down the hallway again. The groupies and the band were gone. They had exited the building.

Security moved through the hallway, ushering the VIP ticket holders, who didn't make the cut, back to the front stage area.

"She'll call if she needs anything, I'm sure," Aria said.

Against my better judgment, I relented. We left the *Garden* and caught a cab back to Aria's apartment.

"I think it's cute the way you look after the people close to you," Aria said. "Even if you are a little uptight."

"I'm not uptight," I said, feeling the tension in my shoulders. "Okay, I'm not usually this uptight. I just feel responsible. I told JD I'd get her back without incident."

"You will." She smiled. "I have no doubt."

She moved close and pressed her full lips against mine. I had forgotten how nice they felt. It didn't take much for Aria to distract my attention. We stumbled into her bedroom with our lips locked, peeling off our clothes along the way.

We fell into bed and reconnected in mind blowing ways. When we had worn ourselves out, she lay beside me with a smooth leg wrapped around me and her head nuzzled into my shoulder.

"I missed you," she said in a delicate breath.

"I missed you too."

"Obviously not *that* much."

"Hey, you were the one that bailed on me."

"It was for work. You know that."

I shrugged.

"It's not like you didn't have fun."

"I don't know if you'd call it fun."

Her eyes narrowed at me. "Please. You banged a movie star."

"A movie star who died!" I said, overstating the obvious.

"Well, that part sucks." She paused. "What was she like?"

It was a little awkward talking to Aria about Bree. "She was nice."

"Did you like her?"

"I didn't get to know her that well."

"But do you think you would have grown to like her?" There was a slight hint of jealousy in her voice.

"Where is this going?"

She shrugged. "I don't know." She paused again. "What if you would have fallen in love with her?"

"That's kind of a moot point, isn't it?"

"Well, what happens when you meet someone? Like, really meet someone?"

"What happens when *you* meet someone?"

She huffed. "You can't answer a question with a question. Honestly, how many girls have you been with since the last time we saw each other?"

"Is this a trick question?"

Her eyes narrowed at me. "No. It's not a trick question. You're free to do whatever you want, I'm just mildly curious?"

"How many guys have *you* been with?" I reconsidered the question immediately. "No. Don't tell me. I don't want to know." I hesitated. "I thought we were doing the no drama, no strings thing?"

She sighed. "Ugh, I don't want to do this."

"Do what?" I asked, hesitantly.

"I'm sorry. I never wanted to fight about this stuff."

"We're not fighting. We're having an... uncomfortable discussion."

She gave me a sour look, not amused. She took a deep breath. "I really like you. You're easy to be around. We have fun together. But our lives are totally different. I *love* New York. I love this city. I love my job!" Her eyes were wide and her face filled with enthusiasm and passion. Then her expression drooped again. "But you're never going to move here, and I couldn't imagine living anywhere else."

"So, we just keep enjoying each other's company when we can." I said, fumbling for words.

"And what? Do that until we each find someone who fits our lives better?"

That hung in the air for a long moment.

I didn't have an answer.

I was saved by a phone call. But it wasn't good news.

32

"**I**'m in trouble," Scarlett stammered, her voice trembling.

"What's going on?" I asked.

"I think they put something in our drinks. I started feeling weird. Sadie doesn't want to leave."

"Where are you now?"

"I locked myself in the bathroom and made myself throw up."

"What room are you in?"

"The penthouse suite. 4100."

"Stay put. I'll be right there."

I launched out of bed and got dressed.

Aria sat up in bed, her face twisted with concern. "What's going on?"

"So much for harmless fun. Stay here. I'll be back shortly."

I caught a cab over to the *King's Court* and stormed into the opulent lobby—marble floors and columns that vaulted to the high ceiling. I marched past the baby grand piano and the waterfall to the elevator bank. I quickly realized I would need a key card to access the 41st floor.

I ran back to the front desk and told them I was the band's manager and had left my key in the room.

The desk clerk looked at me like I was full of shit.

"Look at me. Do I look like a fan?"

The clerk hesitated.

"It's late, and I'm tired, and I have a bunch of assholes to wrangle. And I think they have a few teen girls up there."

I wasn't exactly lying.

He finally programmed a key card and handed it to me. I ran back to the elevator and rocketed up to the 41st floor. The dull thump of music billowed into the hallway.

I ran down the corridor, stuck the card in the key slot, and pushed open the door.

The suite was filled with smoke. There were rock stars and roadies and girls. The foyer opened into a large living area that split the bedrooms.

A big bouncer stomped toward me. He was 6'5", bald, and as thick as a power lifter. A scowl twisted on his face. "Who are you? How did you get in here?"

I punched him in the face, then kneed him in the groin. He doubled over, and I jammed an elbow into the back of his spine.

He flattened to the ground with a groan.

I found the guest bathroom and rapped on the door. "Scarlett? Are you in there?"

"Tyson?"

"Stay there till I come back." I glanced around the living room, looking for Sadie. I didn't see her pink hair anywhere.

"Hey, mother fucker!" the drummer shouted. "Get the fuck out of here before I call the cops!"

"Go ahead. Call them!"

His hands balled into fists, and he looked like he wanted to do something, but he had second thoughts. His eyes flicked to the security guard on the ground, and even in his inebriated state, he realized he didn't stand a chance.

The drummer backed down, and I stormed to the bedroom and kicked open the door. Sadie was passed out on the bed. Zazzle hovered at the foot of the bed, preparing to do something that was too low, even for him.

He slung the hair out of his face and his glassy eyes glared at me. "What the fuck, man?"

I swung a right cross as hard as I could. I'd been waiting to do this since the night I met him in Monaco. My knuckles connected with his jaw, and blood spewed from his lips. His head twisted to the side, and a pearly tooth tumbled from his lips.

Zazzle fell back against the wall and slumped to the ground, out cold.

His teeth against my knuckles hurt, and I shook out my hand.

It was worth the pain.

I climbed onto the bed and tried to wake Sadie. "Come on. Wake up. It's time to go home."

She didn't respond.

My fingertips felt for a pulse on her neck.

It was faint.

Her chest wasn't moving.

I scrambled for my phone and dialed 911.

About that time, the bouncer entered the room, and I found myself on the wrong end of a 9mm. Blood trickled from his nose, dripping down his chin. "Put the phone down!"

"What did you people give her? She OD'd!"

"Put the phone down. We'll deal with this."

"You'll be an accessory to murder. She's not breathing."

He hesitated, then lowered the weapon, realizing this was too big to cover up.

I talked to the 911 operator while starting chest compressions, trying to revive Sadie.

Nothing I did worked, and by the time the EMTs arrived she was gone.

The cops weren't far behind, and everyone was questioned. Several arrests were made. The officers took custody of the body and transferred Sadie to the Medical Examiner where a full autopsy would be performed.

I don't know what they had given her, but it was a central nervous system depressant. It had slowed her breathing to the point where she couldn't function.

Scarlet was dazed and didn't say a word. She stared into the distance blankly. It was almost sunrise by the time we made it back to Aria's apartment. Scarlett made a beeline for the guest bedroom and closed the door behind her. Her muffled sobs filtered through the wall for the next hour.

I caught Aria up to speed on what had happened. She made me breakfast, then I crawled into bed just after sunrise. I needed to get a few hours sleep. When I woke up that afternoon, I called the airline and changed our flight.

I said goodbye to Aria—we'd finish our discussion another time. Scarlett and I caught a cab to LaGuardia, and boarded the 6:15 PM flight to MIA. She would have to miss her meeting with the agent on Tuesday.

I was done with the drama.

We had an hour layover, then caught the last connection to Coconut Key.

It was midnight by the time we got back to JD's. He was in the kitchen making a midnight snack before turning in for the evening.

Scarlett ran into his arms and gave him a big hug. JD winced, still sore from his wound. But that didn't stop him from sharing a nice moment with his daughter.

"I promise, I'm going to stop fucking up," she said.

JD didn't buy it for one minute. "It's your life, kiddo."

"I know."

"I'm just glad you're safe."

Scarlet rolled her suitcase into her bedroom and closed the door.

JD looked to me. "Thanks for bringing her back."

"Anytime."

"Hopefully this is the last time."

"She's a handful, alright."

"You're telling me," JD said.

"Apple doesn't fall far from the tree."

JD glared at me. "She gets it from her mother. Not me."

I had a good laugh at that one.

"Oh, and I hate to break it to you, but you can't stay here anymore."

My jaw dropped. Suddenly, I felt small, like a little kid who had been kicked out of his home. "Uh, okay," I stammered. I tried to play it off like I wasn't hurt. "I was planning on finding a new place, anyway. There are some nice apartments on 23rd Street with a good view of the ocean."

JD dug into his pocket and tossed a set of keys across the room.

I caught them in the palm of my hand. "What's this?"

A wide smile curled on Jack's lips. "My new boat. Your new home."

I regarded him curiously. "What did you buy?"

JD just smiled.

The anticipation was killing me. But I'd have to wait until tomorrow to see his new boat. Tonight, I would crash on the couch.

Ready for more?

Join my newsletter and find out what happens next.

AUTHOR'S NOTE

Thanks for all the great reviews! I'm having such a good time writing Tyson and JD. I can't wait to get started on the next adventure.

If you liked this book, let me know with a review on Amazon.

My Max Mars series is heavy with mystery and thriller elements, you might want to check it out.

Thanks for reading!

—*Tripp*

MAX MARS

The Orion Conspiracy

Blade of Vengeance

The Zero Code

Edge of the Abyss

Siege on Star Cruise 239

Phantom Corps

The Auriga Incident

Devastator

CONNECT WITH ME

I'm just a geek who loves to write. Follow me on Facebook.

www.trippellis.com

Made in the USA
Coppell, TX
25 May 2020

26441756R00129